G000269406

Tangled Affairs

Glenda Stock

Grosvenor House
Publishing Limited

All rights reserved
Copyright © Glenda Stock, 2022

The right of Glenda Stock to be identified as the author of this
work has been asserted in accordance with Section 78
of the Copyright, Designs and Patents Act 1988

The book cover is copyright to Glenda Stock
Cover image – credit to: Spiderplay

This book is published by
Grosvenor House Publishing Ltd
Link House
140 The Broadway, Tolworth, Surrey, KT6 7HT.
www.grosvenorhousepublishing.co.uk

This book is sold subject to the conditions that it shall not, by way of
trade or otherwise, be lent, resold, hired out or otherwise circulated
without the author's or publisher's prior consent in any form of binding or
cover other than that in which it is published and
without a similar condition including this condition being imposed
on the subsequent purchaser.

This book is a work of fiction. Any resemblance to
people or events, past or present, is purely coincidental.

A CIP record for this book
is available from the British Library

ISBN 978-1-83975-966-6

This is dedicated to the lockdowns.
Without them, this book would have
never been completed.

Chapter 1

"Hello, it's me. Are you ready yet?"

"I'm nearly ready Angela. I'm just in the loo. I don't want to be caught short. I know how far you make me walk on our regular hikes. Those bushes can be too prickly to go behind for a wee," laughed Caroline.

"I fancy walking in Elm Woods today. Do you? It's a lovely day and it will be completely dry underfoot. No need for wellies or hiking boots."

"Will we be ok with trainers?"

"Yes, I have got mine on. You must be out of that bathroom by now. You won't need that cardigan. Where is your sense of adventure? Live dangerously. The temperature is going to reach the 80's today. We are so lucky that we don't have to slave away over a hot computer. Why do women who are married to rich men feel the need to have to go out to work? Do you agree, Caroline? Look at the lives we lead. We can do what we want to when we want to. I wouldn't change that for a power suit and shoulder pads."

"Yes, Angela, I agree but, not everyone is the same."

Caroline always agreed with her friend Angela. Angela was the sort of person who it is best to agree with. It saved a lot of time and trouble. Angela was right about the cardigan. Caroline could be a little over cautious. Angela could never be accused of being over cautious. In some ways Caroline could be very reckless but, only Angela knew that side of her. Caroline and Angela were both keen walkers and did spend a lot of time doing this activity together. Of course, she would walk in Elm Woods today. After all, Angela had suggested it.

"Will we need a picnic?" enquired Caroline.

"Don't be silly. It may be a scorching hot day but, I am not sitting down in the middle of the footpath with a fish paste sandwich. Just bring water. We will go to the pub for lunch. If you don't get a move on it will be lunch time."

The two women set off on their hike. They were laughing like schoolgirls and enjoying their freedom and the hot, sunny day. It wasn't far to the gate that led them to the woods. It was only at the back of the Barker's End estate where they both lived. Angela and Caroline had met when they both moved into a house on the estate on the same day. They were different in many ways including personality and lifestyle. Caroline had been married to Nick for ten years. She had two daughters aged eight and six years. She has never wanted to be a working Mum and felt fortunate that Nick earned enough for her to be able to be a housewife and mother. Angela is married to Chris and is adamant that she will never have a child. Chris is a solicitor and Angela spends a lot of time helping him entertain his clients. Despite her glamorous lifestyle, compared to Caroline's, she is a very loyal friend to Caroline and is always willing to look after her children.

"You're right about me not needing that cardigan. I'm sweltering."

"What did I tell you? You know your Auntie Angela always knows best."

The two friends had walked quite a few miles so stopped for a drink of water. Caroline was surveying the landscape and about to suggest that they took a particular path when Angela interrupted her thoughts.

"Should we take the path to the left? I don't think that we have tried that way before."

"Oh, I was just about to suggest that we go straight on and turn off to the left at the next fork," said Caroline, rather irritated that her friend had yet again made the decision.

"No, we don't want to go that way. Mandy Robinson went that way with her family last weekend and, they got covered in stinging nettles. We have only got our shorts on. No, I think my way is best."

"Yes, all right then. You know best. I don't think that we have turned left before. We won't get lost, will we? You know I must pick the girls up before five. We are lucky that we have extra time today as they go to after school club. I feel a bit guilty, actually. I am not a working Mum so there is no need for them to go to the club but, they say they enjoy it and most of their friends, whose Mums do work, go there."

"Caroline, stop beating yourself up. You are a brilliant mother to those girls. I might hate kids but, if I had to have any they would have to be just like your Sophie and Millie. Anyway, we need that extra time today for the pub."

As Caroline and Angela continued along the footpath they came to the section where many shrubs lined the footpaths. They both agreed that they had never walked that way before and it was a good idea.

The wild summer flowers had carpeted the ground. Daisies, geraniums, all sorts of little, delicate blooms covered the whole field. The ladies had no idea what most of the plants were called but, they didn't care. Everywhere looked so lovely. They never knew why it was called Elm Wood as it wasn't much of a wood. Woods were supposed to be full of trees. Elm Wood was more fields with bushes running alongside the footpaths. The footpaths had been man made by the local council. They weren't proper tarmac or concrete pavements. They were just cleared of bushes. It was still very muddy in wet weather but, the paths were part of the local authorities plan to encourage health and fitness as well as family bonding for the residents. Caroline preferred the wild flowers. Trees, she thought, were creepy and she is not sure if she would venture out into the woods, even in daylight, if it had been full of trees.

"Angela, look that bush up there looks as though someone has fallen into it."

"Well, could be a drunk stumbled on the way home from the pub or, you do get a lot of kids in here messing about at night. So, it could be one of those simple explanations. I don't think it is anything for us to worry about. Not even you." Angela laughed. "If you really want me to, I will put on my detective hat and investigate. Davies of The Yard and the case of the Dented Bush."

"All right, very clever. I only mentioned it because it is rather a large bush and it is very noticeable that something has happened to it. It's all caved in."

"Caroline, come here. There is something. I don't like the look of."

"I do believe you are scared, Angela Davies. Now who is the cautious one? Should I investigate for Chief Inspector Davies?"

"Seriously Caroline. Come quickly. Look at this. I think some old tramp is asleep in here."

"Leave him Angela. He could be dangerous. He might be violent. We are out here alone. Let's go back now. We could take our usual short cut. Never mind the footpath that takes us to the Elm Arms. I just want to get back now."

"Oh, do shut up Caroline. Calm down. There are plenty of dog walkers and cyclists using these footpaths. We are hardly alone. Anyway, you are supposed to be the compassionate one. He may need medical attention."

"Yes, I see your point. I am getting my mobile out of my bag ready to call the police or Nick. I'm going to see what other rubbish I have in my bag. I may have something heavy to hit him with, if need be."

"Well, let's be brave. I'll go first, shall I?" Yes, I thought so. Caroline, I'm sure he's not breathing and, I don't think he is a tramp. He is smartly dressed. Caroline, my God. I'm going to be sick. It's Paul."

"What, Paul? Whose Paul? What do you mean he is not breathing? Angela you are really terrifying me now. Stop messing about. This is no time for your jokes. Where are you? Should I call Nick and Chris? Should I call the police, ambulance? Angela, where are you? I don't know what to do."

Angela appeared from the other side of the dented bush. Her face appeared to be drained of colour. Even her suntan had faded. Her body was shivering, and she didn't speak to her friend.

"Angela?"

"I told you I was sick. It's Paul and he is dead."

Caroline was sobbing. She still hadn't seen this body for herself and she told her friend that she didn't know who Paul was and, knew even less about why he was lying dead in a bush.

"Caroline, you do know Paul. The odd-job man from the village."

"Paul. That Paul? He can't be dead. How do you know that he is dead? You're not a doctor. Don't touch him. I'm phoning the police. Police please."

"Where exactly are you Madam?"

"I don't know. It's in the woods. I'm with my friend. We were just walking. I don't have a clue where we are. Oh, wait a minute. The footpath leads back into the village. Barker's End. Yes, they will find us, won't they?" I hope they are not too long. What should we do?"

"There is nothing we can do. We can't do anything for poor old Paul."

"Why is he dead? Did someone kill him or was he drunk? He did like his drink but, it wouldn't kill him. Would it? Was he ill?"

"Caroline, stop asking all of these ridiculous questions. I'm not really Davies of the Yard, you know. We will have to wait."

"Do we have to wait for the police to arrive?"

"Of course we do. We found the body. They will have to question us."

"We haven't done anything wrong. I said we should have taken the other path."

"You are being hysterical now. They always question the person who finds the body. Don't you watch Morse or Midsomer Murders? Why are you so afraid? If we had taken the other footpath someone else would have found him. Poor old Paul is still dead. Have a drink of water. It's a pity we are not in the pub. We could both do with a brandy."

"Well ladies, perhaps you could answer a few questions."

The policeman was very polite and, Caroline realised how panic-stricken she had been. The water seemed to have calmed her down or, at least, gave her something to focus on to stop her hands from shaking. The police would know straight away that neither she nor Angela could have anything to do with Paul's death. It's probably just an accident. Paul did drink too much. Well, that's what the village gossips had told her.

"Oh, my God. I completely forgot about the girls. I must telephone the school. What time is it?"

"I'll get Chris to collect them. Nick can't get to the school in time. Chris doesn't have any appointments today. It won't be any trouble for him," Angela reassured Caroline.

"Thank you, Angela. I wish I was calm and always in control like you," replied a grateful Caroline.

"So, you both knew this gentleman, did you?"

"Not very well. Everyone in the village knew Paul. He had probably worked on everyone's house at some time or other. You knew him better than I did, Caroline? Your Nick was going to get a quote from him for your garage."

"Yes, Nick did get a quote from him. I don't think he was going to employ him, though," replied Caroline hesitantly.

"Do you know why that was, Mrs Freeman? Was there any disagreement?"

"What do you mean? No of course not. I think Nick had other quotes to consider." Caroline was anxious as she was convinced that the police officer thought she had something to hide.

"Thank you, ladies. That will be all for now. We have your names and addresses if we require you to answer any further questions."

"What does he mean, any more questions? We only found the body. We could have ignored it and let someone else phone the police. You should have listened to me for once, Angela. If we had taken the pathway that I had suggested none if this would have happened."

"Calm down, Caroline. That is very public spirited of you, I don't think. Let someone else find the body. Paul may not have been your best friend but, the man is dead and, we did find the body so that's it. Why are you feeling so guilty? I never thought of you being a murderer," Angela laughed.

"How can you even think of laughing at a time like this?"

"Look, I am as shocked as you are. I probably knew Paul better than you did but, we are not going to bring him back by crying."

"You told that policeman that I knew him better but, he had worked on your house. Why would you say that?"

"Look Caroline. I didn't mean anything. Just that Nick had asked him about your garage quite recently."

Angela and Caroline walked home briskly and in silence. Angela was feeling more shocked than she had revealed by their gruesome discovery. Caroline's only concern now was the welfare of her children. Had Chris collected them from school?

"Look Angela, Chris has got the girls. I have never been so relieved in my life."

"I told you that Chris would have it all in hand. He won't admit it but, he loves spending time with Sophie and Millie. That is one thing you can stop fretting about now."

"Hello you two. Are you all right?"

"Why shouldn't we be all right Mum? Chris didn't tell us what had happened. We think it must be something exciting for you not to collect us from school. Is it exciting, Mummy? Is it a crime? Will the police have to come to our house? Chris took us for a burger. I wasn't supposed to tell you that bit. Chris isn't in trouble for buying us junk food, is he Mummy?" asked Sophie.

"No Sophie. Chris isn't in trouble. I can't thank him enough for looking after you. I need a burger myself. Angela and I haven't eaten since breakfast. I haven't heard from your Dad. Chris you haven't heard from Nick, have you? He is probably driving on some motorway miles from home. I hope he gets home soon."

Caroline picked up her phone, hoping that it was Nick.

"Hello, yes, I'm ok but, I can't really speak now. I will phone you back, bye." Come on you two. I need a drink. Are you and Chris coming in Angela?"

"No thanks, Caroline. I think I will just prepare a quick salad for our dinner. I will pop round later for that drink, though."

As Angela leaves Caroline she hears her on the phone.

"This is really a bad time for talking now. After I have got the girls to bed I will give you a ring."

"Sophie, Millie time for bed. No excuses. You have had a treat for tea. There is no time for a bath tonight. A quick shower will do. I don't want any arguments. I have had enough today."

"Mum."

"What did I just say? Your Dad will be home, soon and I'll send him up to see you."

"It's not fair."

"Please just do as you are told. You will know all about what happened soon."

Caroline sat down with a large glass of wine. She knew it was a mistake as she had no food inside her to keep her clear-headed. She deserved a drink. She would deserve another when Angela visited. Firstly, she must call James.

"I can talk now but, Nick isn't home yet. I don't know how long he will be. I suppose you have heard about my eventful day."

"I have got some news for you Caroline. I am working on the case. I didn't want too but, I had no choice. They do know that you and I are acquainted but you're not a suspect so there won't be any problems. You didn't kill him, did you?" laughed James.

"Very funny. I did feel like a suspect when the police arrived at the scene this afternoon. Just a minute. I think Angela has just come in the back door. I will have to go."

"Are you still leaving that door unlocked? There is possibly a murderer on the loose. We won't know that, of course until we get the forensic results but, I thought you, of all people, would be more careful."

"Right, I will lock the door but, I must go."

"Hello Angela. Come in. I will pour us a glass of wine."

"Who was that on the phone? Was it James? He called earlier, didn't he?"

"Yes. I am sure you knew that. That is why you came here this evening. You weren't really concerned about my welfare."

"Hang on a minute. It was obvious that it was James on the phone when we were all outside. I just didn't want you to have something else to worry about. Is James coming round to see you?"

"I'm sorry Angela. I just can't cope with all of this drama. No, James isn't coming here. He did tell me that he has been assigned to Paul's case, though. They don't know that it is murder, for sure. I don't think that they would know who is going to be conducting the enquiries if they were not pretty sure that it was murder, do you?"

"It's good that James will be doing all of the questioning. It will make it easier for you when he comes asking questions. A friendly face. Do they know that you and James are childhood friends?"

"Yes but, as I am not involved it doesn't matter."

"Well, that's good then."

"I don't like the way you said that Angela. You don't think that I am involved in any of this, do you?"

"Don't be so silly. Look all of this has affected you badly. Go to bed and get some sleep. Perhaps we can go shopping in town tomorrow. There is nothing like a bit of retail therapy to cheer us up."

"I'll see how I feel. I don't want to go to bed until Nick gets home. I have forgotten to try his mobile. I will call him now. Goodnight Angela." Caroline sat, wearily down, after double locking the doors and making sure every window in the house was secure.

"Nick, thank God you have answered at last. Where have you been?"

"Caroline, what's up? You sound dreadful. It's not one of the girls? Are they ok?"

"The girls are fine, sound asleep. How long will you be? I'll tell you everything when you get home."

"Are you all right love? I've been stuck on the motorway. There were a couple of accidents. I didn't like to use the mobile even though I wasn't moving an inch. There were too many police around. What's happened? Why couldn't I get in? Have we had a break-in?"

Caroline recalled the events of the day. Nick was visibly shocked by what his wife had told him.

"Don't bother getting me anything to eat. I will just make a sandwich. I don't know about you but, I need a drink. He is the chap that came here to do the garage, isn't he? I can't say I liked the bloke. Do they think it was an accident?"

"They don't know, yet. I think they are treating his death as suspicious. James is going to investigate. If there is anything to investigate. Angela worried me when she spoke to the police. She told them that you had not employed Paul to do the garage. The police implied that you and Paul may have had a disagreement. Do you think that they think that you killed him?"

"I think that you are very stressed and imagining all sorts of scenarios. If he was murdered they will come and question me. It's obvious. They will question everyone who knows him." Nick stared into his wine glass, thoughtfully, before taking the last gulp of the liquid.

"Caroline, I have got to go away for a few days. They need me in Birmingham to do a presentation for some clients from China. I know it's bad timing but, this was all planned today. I really didn't know that Paul was going to get himself killed."

"When do you have to go? What if the police want to speak to you? What am I going to do without you?"

"Just a minute. Hang on. One question at a time. I am going tomorrow afternoon. I am sure the police can wait for three days. You will have Angela and the girls to keep you company."

"You know very well what I mean. I don't want to be without you at a time like this. There could be a murderer roaming the village. He may break into the house and kill us all."

"Caroline, calm down. It is very unlikely that a serial killer is loose in this community. Paul was probably drunk and had an accident. Anyway, this house is like Fort Knox. I have been away before. You always say that you like the peace."

"Yes, I know. I'm sorry. I don't want you to think that you have a hysterical, clingy wife. Angela and Chris will be there if I need them. You know Angela. She loves a crisis and likes to take charge. I will go upstairs to make sure you have enough ironed shirts."

Angela visited her friend the next day.

"When did you say Nick was coming back?" asked Angela.

"I didn't but, he will be back on Friday. Why?" questioned Caroline.

"I don't know what you are worried about. You have never cared when he went on business trips before. Oh, I get it. Does this Paul business change your nice little set-up you had with a certain person?"

"I don't really want to discuss this now. I must collect the girls from school and then Nick will be home for his bag. See you tomorrow," Caroline was hurrying away from her friend. She had another visitor. I can't take all of these people, she sighed, to herself.

"Hello James. Has there been any news about Paul? Was it an accident? Nick said that would probably be the most likely explanation for his death."

"Has Nick gone away?"

"Yes, James but, how did you know?"

"I saw Angela and she told me you might need some company. You know, an old friend to cheer you up."

"I don't know. All the excitement during the last few days has made me tired. Oh, why not. An old school friend is just what I need. We can discuss the past. It will be a lot more pleasant than thinking about the present. I will put the kettle on. I know that you won't even have one drink when you are driving. You don't mind if I have a glass of wine, do you? I will just go and pour out your tea."

"It's good to see you. I've got some news. Paul was murdered. It's not a secret as it will be in the local papers and on the television tomorrow. I did tell you that I will be working on the case, didn't I?"

"Yes, you did but, I didn't really think it would be a murder enquiry. We don't have murders here. Nick was wrong then. There is a murderer on the loose in Barker's End. I need another drink."

"I shouldn't be telling you this but, we think the killer was targeting Paul. We don't think that there is a serial killer on the loose so, you can sleep easy without the help of the wine bottle."

"Are you telling me how much to drink, now? What gives you the right? Just because you joined the police force you are no better than me. Why would anyone kill Paul?"

"I'm really trying to help, Caroline. You have to get the girls from school, and you need to carry on as normal. Have a nap before you pick them up."

"Normal. Why shouldn't we carry on as normal. I have done nothing wrong. I was just the unlucky sod who found the body. Well, that's not true. Angela found the body but, good old Angela. She can cope with anything."

"I think I will go now, Caroline. I will call and see you another day. Perhaps you can stick to tea when we next meet. My boss will need to question you and Nick. I can make some excuse if you would rather I didn't accompany him. My superiors know that we are old school friends, so it's up to you."

"Why are they going to question us?"

"We have to question nearly everyone in the village. We don't really know anything about Paul Robertson. We don't even have a next of kin. Now, just get some sleep and try and keep calm. See you soon."

After James had left her alone in the house Caroline couldn't help thinking about the remark that Angela has made earlier. Were the police going to question Nick because of the disagreement over the price of the garage repairs? She lay awake that night. Was she scared of the impending questions or, the fact that if Nick could be wrong about Paul's death being an accident, he could be wrong about the house being secure?

It can't be the alarm clock, already, thought Caroline. She must get up and sort out the girls.

"It's my turn to have the chocolate cereal. Mum, Sophie has taken it all. It's not fair."

"Millie, please be quiet. Sophie, you knew it was her turn. We can all go shopping, in the car, after school. Dad was picked up, so I can have the car, today. I will get you the cereal of your choice. I didn't sleep last night. I don't want any arguments whilst your dad is away."

"Dad has been away loads of times. Did you have too much wine last night, Mummy?"

"No, I didn't and I'm just a bit tired. Please, both of you, do as you are told."

"Why don't you ask Auntie Angela to take us to school or, perhaps we could go in Uncle Chris's car. His car is brilliant, and it goes really fast."

"I will take you to school. Eat your breakfast. Get your bags. You won't need a jacket. Come on let's just go."

When Caroline turned the corner into the close after taking the girls to school she saw Angela weeding her front garden. She really didn't want to see Angela today but, there was no avoiding her.

"Just let me finish this and I will call round for coffee. You look as though you need coffee."

"Thanks, Angela. I really need to be told that I look terrible. See you soon."

Caroline must tidy the house and put some clothes in the washing machine. If Angela sees that house is a mess she will know that she is not coping with the recent events. Angela can cope with everything. The last thing that Caroline wants is for Angela to feel sorry for her and take control.

"Did I see James's car here, yesterday?"

"I think you know what James's car looks like, and you told James that I needed cheering up, so if you think you saw it here you probably did." I really must stop being so grumpy, thought Caroline. Irritability is the first sign that I can't handle it. Angela will spot that instantly.

"Sorry Angela. I had a few glasses of wine last night. You know me. Two glasses and I can't sleep. Coffee? That will sort me out."

"I suppose you have seen the paper or, did James tell you?"

"He did tell me, actually. He said it would be in the media today so there was no harm in letting me know. I think that a murderer roaming the streets was partly the reason that I didn't sleep. Not just the wine."

"I don't think you need to worry about a murderer. I think that Paul was the target. Paul wasn't perfect. That is what I have heard anyway."

"James said that. He said that Paul was probably killed because of an argument. You should join the police force, you know. You have all of the answers, Inspector Davies."

What Caroline had to admit to herself that she did feel better after coffee and a chat. She knew Angela was a good friend. In fact, Angela had inspired her to go and weed her own garden. Gardening always helped Caroline cope with her problems. It was very therapeutic. She would just get the front garden hoed and then it would be time to collect the girls.

"Hello, Caroline."

Oh, thought Caroline. How could she avoid a long conversation with Hilary? Caroline may have thought that she didn't want Angela's company today but, she knew Angela was a true friend. Hilary was just a playground gossip.

"Caroline, have you heard the news? Did you know that Paul was murdered? Have the police questioned

Nick yet? I bet you're worried. Your Nick was the last person to have a disagreement with Paul. I know a lot of the men round here have had rows with Paul but, he didn't end up dead then, did he?"

"I'm not at all worried, Hilary. Nick is just as incapable of murder as I am. As you said, many people have argued with Paul. Nick was only haggling over the price of some repairs," replied Caroline sounding more confident than she felt. I must go now, Hilary. I have got some shopping to do."

Caroline had collected the girls in the car to shop, as promised but, she knew that she shouldn't really be driving. Nick would go mad if he thought the girls were in the car with her in this state.

"What are you doing, Mum? You nearly hit that car."

"I was nowhere near that car, Sophie. When you are old enough to drive you are welcome to go to the supermarket."

"Sorry," replied Sophie sarcastically.

Caroline knew that she had nearly hit the car in the supermarket car park. She wasn't concentrating. How did Hilary know about Paul, Nick and the garage? Why was this all so important? Did anyone have a grudge against Nick?

Caroline couldn't think of a reason why anyone would want to implicate Nick in a murder. He always seemed so popular. When he wasn't away, he played cricket for the village team. He shared a joke with the pub regulars. He was a good husband. The girls adored him. The conversation with Hilary had, once again, shattered her confidence. Why hadn't they taken the other footpath in the woods?

Chapter 2

"Why don't I stay for another coffee? Or would you rather have something stronger? There is nothing we can do. You will just have to wait until Nick gets back and the police question him."

"Angela, you know that Nick can't possibly have anything to do with this. He would never even kill a spider. He has never even stolen a pen from the office. He only uses his mobile phone in the car when he is in a lay-by. Well, yes, I know he phoned me the other evening when he was on the motorway but, he was stationary. Angela, you know it wasn't him."

"Calm down Caroline. I think you need a brandy. Forget the coffee. All I said was that the police will question Nick because he and Paul had an argument about the price of the garage repairs. It's obvious that they will ask him questions. If he is innocent what is all the fuss about?"

"What do you mean, if? Forget the brandy and the coffee. I thought that you were my friend. You are just as bad as that Hilary woman. See you around, Angela," said Caroline as she opened the door for her friend.

"Wait, Caroline. I am your friend, and you need me now more than ever. You know me and my big mouth. I don't think before I speak. Now let's have a drink and think about this logically. We found the body. We can solve the crime. Who would want to kill Paul?"

Angela managed to persuade Caroline that she should stay and finish the rather large brandy that she had poured. The two women could not think of anyone who would actually kill Paul. Paul could be aggressive after a few drinks but, so could a lot of men. Many of the local men didn't like him. This was probably because he wasn't one of the lads. He didn't mix much and wasn't part of the cricket, darts, drinking set.

What did they know about him? Nothing thought Caroline. Did he have a wife or mother? Did he have a girlfriend? Caroline sat thoughtfully clinging on to her glass.

"Nick, thank God. Home at last."

"Don't worry I'll see myself out," yelled Angela from the front door.

"Caroline, love. I have only been gone a couple of days. I said I would be back today. How are the girls?"

"The girls are fine. Same as always. I'll make a cup of tea. Let me unpack your case and I will put your clothes in the washing machine."

"You don't have to do that now. Just the tea will be fine. One thing at a time."

"I want to get it over with. You haven't got anything to hide in that case, have you?"

"What's wrong? What would I be hiding from you?"

"I'm sorry, Nick. I just can't cope with all of this drama. You see Angela and I found Paul. He was dead. I just know that the police have got to question you. I'm scared Nick."

"Sit down. I know you found him but, that was just unfortunate for you both. Have a cup of tea with me. You know that a cup of tea is always the answer to a crisis."

Caroline tried to smile at Nick's light hearted handling of the situation but, nothing could stop the anxiety that had overwhelmed her. She knew that Nick was innocent but, she couldn't stop worrying. Just as Nick was calming her down, there was a knock at the door.

"Nick Freeman? Hello Sir. I'm Detective Chief Inspector Stock. This is Detective Sergeant Watson. Can we come in?"

"Yes, please take a seat. I know the sergeant. How are you, James? I know what this is all about. I have been expecting you. I'm glad that you are here. My wife has been rather nervous since she discovered the body with Angela. She may be able to relax after you realize that I had nothing to do with the death of this man. Would you like a cup of tea? What do you want to know?"

"Thank you, Mr. Freeman. Milk and two sugars for both of us please, oh make that three sugars for me. So far, we have little information concerning Mr. Robertson's home life or acquaintances. It is known that Mr. Robertson and you argued on the day that he came to this house. Perhaps you would tell us what happened that day."

"I wouldn't say that we argued. I didn't like Paul Robertson but, a lot of men in the village felt the same way. Paul could be argumentative and aggressive after he had been drinking. He wasn't one of us. We didn't know him really. A few friends had recommended him to me. Although he wasn't popular, he was considered to be very good at his job. I needed a new door on the garage and some shelves. When Paul gave me his quote I knew that he was charging too much. I told him that he must be joking and that I would go somewhere else. Paul, being Paul, got a bit shirty and told me I wouldn't get it done any cheaper anywhere else or, to such a high standard. He then left. That's all, really."

"You didn't hit Mr. Robertson?"

"Of course I didn't hit him. I don't go around hitting people. Anyone will tell you that. I told you he just left. Has anyone told you any different?"

"What makes you ask that, Mr. Freeman?"

"It's nothing. It's just that my wife has heard gossip from the other mums. You know, just playground tittle-tattle. She has been upset by all of this and the rumours haven't helped. I just thought that someone might have it in for me."

"Can you think of anyone that might bear such a grudge that they would want to implicate you in a murder Sir?"

"No, no of course not. Caroline has got this all out of proportion."

"Well, that's all for now Mr. Freeman. We will be in touch if we need to ask you further questions."

Caroline had listened to the conversation between the police and her husband from the kitchen. She knew that she ought to be grateful that he hadn't been arrested and taken away but, she had this niggling feeling that they would be back.

"I think he is hiding something."

"What makes you think that, Watson?"

"I don't know. Just an instinct. I think he is a bit too nice and a bit too clever,"

"I don't think we can charge a man for murder on instinct, even yours Watson. Being clever and nice are rather good qualities and, they are not illegal, yet."

The next morning they were all there, in a huddle in the playground. The women that she hated. Caroline is muttering to herself.

Oh, god, not the Mums set. The perfect mothers with their perfect lives. The coffee mornings after the school run; the afternoon tea or, wine when the children are playing happily together after school. It's alright for Angela. She revels in the attention from the other women. And she's not even a Mum. I hate it. I am the centre of attention now, or rather my husband is, and for all the wrong reasons. Should I smile and say I have to be somewhere by 9.30am? No, they won't believe me. Should I change the subject? What other subject is there to discuss in the village? Be brave and ready for the interrogation.

"Caroline, how lovely to see you. How calm and relaxed you look, under the circumstances."

Vicky is such a bitch at the best of times. All three of her children are top of the class, academically. They are all in the sports teams and could set up a whole orchestra amongst themselves.

"Hello, Vicky. I really have got to get back early today." What happened to the bravery?

"Are the police coming to question Nick, again?"

"No, whatever gave you that idea? It's just that with all the excitement the house has been neglected. A lot to do. You know how it is."

Vicky, of course, had no idea, how it is. As well as brilliant children, she also employs a cleaner. Vicky has been joined by Hilary and Jackie. When an anxious

Caroline gets back to her home she telephones Angela to ask her a favour.

"Angela, can you do something for me? It is a massive favour."

"Of course, what is it?"

"You are going to think I am an absolute wimp but, can you take the girls to and from school until this murder business is all cleared up? My husband isn't a murderer. I really don't think I can face any of them. Especially, Hilary, Jackie and Vicky. You know I'm just not one of them at the best of times."

"You know I will do anything for you and the girls but, really Caroline you mustn't let them get to you even if Nick is guilty. You have done nothing wrong."

"What do you mean, if Nick is guilty? You keep saying if. How can you seriously think that he could kill anyone? Don't bother with the girls. I will get Mum and Dad to come and stay. In fact, don't bother contacting me again. With friends like you, who needs enemies."

After Caroline had finished speaking to Angela and thrown down the phone in anger, she poured herself a glass of wine. How has it come to this? Drinking before 10am. Coffee time. As she felt the wine was calming her nerves the doorbell rang. Will it be Angela coming to apologise? Perhaps, the police. I must pour the wine away. I don't want them to think I am turning to drink because I know that Nick is guilty. Caroline could see through the glass door that her visitor wasn't Angela or the police. It was James.

"Can I come in, Caroline? I am not on duty. This is a social call. I am not disturbing you, am I?"

"No, come in. Tea, coffee? I have just got back from the school."

"I will have coffee. It looks as though you need one yourself. The wine really won't help, you know. I only want to look after you, Caroline. You know how I feel about you. I've always loved you. I know that I didn't always show it. I just put my career first. It didn't mean that I loved you less. I shouldn't have given up without a fight when you met Nick. I was stupid."

Caroline knew what this would lead to. She wasn't thinking about Nick or the girls. She put both of the coffee cups down on the table and moved closer to James on the settee. She, gently, kissed James on the lips.

James held her hand and led Caroline up the stairs to the bedroom that she shared with Nick. Caroline knew this wasn't right, especially with Nick under suspicion of murder but, James was what she needed. Not only had he been her lover for a long time but, she felt he was her only friend. As he laid her on the bed and kissed her the stress and guilt disappeared. She ripped off his clothes and the passion and excitement as he removed her underwear was almost more than she could take. Nothing in her life could make her feel the way she did like making love with James. He was gentle, kind but, passionate and exciting. This was her pleasure in life. This made her feel as exciting as her friend, Angela. Only Angela knew about her affair. Angela: she felt guilty about what she had said earlier. As she got dressed and James kissed her goodbye her fears returned. How could she do this to Nick? He was going to need her now, more than ever. What about the girls? She had no intention of leaving Nick for James and splitting up her family. No, James was just a diversion. Bored housewife syndrome. This affair must always be a secret. Angela was her ally, her confident. She must apologise, she must see her now.

"Hello Caroline, do you still want me to collect the girls from school? I am quite happy to go up to the school soon."

"Angela, how could you still be so nice to me after what I said this morning? I have come to apologise."

"What are friends for? I know that you are under a lot of pressure. Come on, we have time for a cup of tea, and we will walk to the school, together."

Angela; dependable, confident. She has loads of friends and male admirers. Why is her friendship with Caroline so important to her? Caroline had often had these thoughts and could put the reason down to two possibilities. Angela was a genuinely nice person who genuinely liked Caroline or, Caroline made her look even more fabulous. No, I must not think like this. Angela has never let me down.

The police can find no real motive for Paul's murder. They can't find any living relatives, partners, ex- wives or anyone close to him. He lived in a rented flat in the nearby town of Newston. Paul's landlady identified the body, always clutching her handkerchief to her face.

"He was a good lad, not trouble at all," she sobbed as she was led away.

Paul had no police record, no points on his driving licence and had a good credit rating. He had travelled around the country and worked wherever he could. He had never claimed un-employment benefit and he didn't seem to have any family. He was a man of mystery.

Meanwhile, Caroline was at home. I must lose myself in a practical task. I will cook something for dinner, find that recipe. I must concentrate. I haven't made this for ages.

"Is that you, Nick? I am glad you're home. I have had time, today, to prepare a really nice dinner. Your favourite. Come in now girls, Dad is home, wash your hands, dinner in five minutes."

"Thanks, I'm starving and that looks delicious. Come on girls, up the table. Look what Mum has cooked."

"I don't like that. I went off it last week," moaned Sophie.

"That's disgusting," said Millie as she walked away from the dining table.

"Don't eat it, go to bed, both of you. Just go. I don't want to see either of you until morning."

Caroline was hysterical, screaming the words to her daughters, with tears rolling down her cheeks and into her mouth. If Nick hadn't have been there she was sure she would have hit both girls, uncontrollably.

"Just calm down. Sit and eat. They may not like it but, we are going to sit and eat this in peace. I will go up and see them later. What's got into you? I have never seen you like this."

"I am so sorry. I wanted this meal to be special. They are all whispering behind my back, all the other Mums. Those nasty bitches that hang around in the playground. They all think that you murdered Paul. What are we going to do, Nick? Did you kill him in the garage that day he came here? Did you put his body in the woods? Did he provoke you? I can't cope with this any longer. Go to the police and confess. Tell them in was in self-defence. You won't be in prison for long. At least it will all be over."

"What are you talking about? Do you really think that I am capable of murdering a man because I didn't agree with his quote? You really need to calm down. You will make yourself very ill, Caroline. Should I go and fetch Angela? Perhaps she could talk some sense into you. Perhaps you should make an appointment at the surgery. Get some sedatives."

"I don't know what's happening to me. You are right. Pills will help until this is all over."

Caroline made an appointment at the doctor's surgery. Her GP agreed that she should be prescribed sedatives for a short time. Caroline slept well. Thank God the pills were working. Nick telephoned work the next day to say he wouldn't be in because of a domestic crisis. He realised that Caroline finding the body had caused the extra pressure on her and he didn't, for one minute, really think that she thought him guilty of murder. He took the girls to school. They were concerned about their mother but, he smoothed over the situation.

Caroline seemed a lot calmer in the days that followed her dinner-time outburst. She seemed to accept that Nick was innocent and with his and Angela's help even managed to ignore the gossips. She took the girls to and from school and just managed a cheery greeting to the playground gang. Angela helped to give her confidence. The murder hadn't been solved but, the village resigned itself to this fact and life returned to normal. Caroline had ended her affair with James. Why did she even start it? What was she thinking? Life seemed better, until a visit one evening. She didn't need extra visitors. Every knock at the door scared her. Was it the murderer? Was it the police?

"Good evening, Mrs Freeman, is your husband in," asked DCI Stock, as he stood in the doorway.

"No, sorry, what do you want him for, he's away, why do you want to talk to him?" Caroline's words tumbled out and she knew that if she continued to talk she would sound hysterical and, more importantly, guilty. "Do come in, Chief Inspector: tea, coffee?"

"Tea would be just the job, three sugars. I know that's far too much but, you know, this job, the sugar helps me think. No, I suppose you don't know. Anyway, your husband, Mrs Freeman. When will he be back?"

"Friday, why, he's not a murderer. What do you want to question him for?"

"Please stay calm, Mrs Freeman. We don't know anything about Mr. Robertson, the victim, that's his name. Did you know? Yes of course you did. He doesn't appear to have any relatives. We don't know where he was before he came to Newston. We just have to question anyone who knew anything, and your husband was the last person to speak to Mr. Robertson. Well, at least, the last person to have a disagreement with him."

"Sorry, please ignore me, really sorry. It's just finding the body and everything. I've never seen a body. I don't suppose many people have. Really sorry for going on. More tea?"

"Don't worry, Mrs Freeman. I would love more tea but, I should be getting on. I'll phone Friday to make sure that Mr Freeman is back and, try not to worry. I'll let myself out."

"Thank you, see you Friday."

What did she mean, thank you see you Friday. This wasn't going to be a social visit. They think that Nick murdered Paul. What am I going to do?

"What did that man want, Mummy?" came a voice from upstairs.

"Nothing, go back to sleep. He just wanted to speak to Daddy."

"Have you had too much wine again, Mummy? You sound cross. Are you still tired?"

"I haven't had any wine. I will be up in a minute. Do you want some water? Everything will be all right when Daddy gets back."

Caroline knew that wasn't true. Everything was going to get a lot worse. She told Nick to expect visitors when he got home.

"Good of you to see us, Mr. Freeman. As I told your wife, we don't have any clues, at the moment, to who would want to kill Mr Robertson. Please tell us what you can remember of the meeting with Mr. Robertson that took place here regarding some work on your garage."

"Of course, I told you everything when you first called round."

"Yes but, just a bit more detail please Mr. Freeman."

"Well, as you probably know Paul, Mr Roberston, was a general handyman and a lot of the village had hired him for work. I heard, down the pub, that he was very good so, I asked him here to give me a quote on a new garage door. I wanted some shelves in there as well, Caroline will tell you, I am useless at DIY. Isn't that right, love."

Caroline didn't reply. She just giggled, nervously.

"I had a rough idea of the costs of this type of work so, when Paul gave me a verbal quote, I knew the price was far too high. I told him this and he threw down his tape measure and told me to get someone else and not to waste his time again. I did respond and told him the idea of obtaining quotes is to get the best price for the work. I couldn't understand what had made him so angry. He must have had been refused jobs before. I can only think that the work had dried up and he was desperate for money. Anyway, as he left the garage he shoved me and I fell onto the lawnmower. I am not a violent man in any way, Inspector. Ask Caroline. I just couldn't stand his attitude and retaliated. He wasn't hurt. He just fell backwards. I don't think anyone had actually stood up to him before. That's it. I told him that I was getting another quote. A bloke is coming round tomorrow, is what I told him. That's the end of it. Why am I going to murder someone who I didn't employ? He doesn't owe me money. Nothing has been lost. Is that it, Inspector?"

"You didn't tell us that you attacked Mr Robertson."

"I wouldn't say attacked, just a gentle shove," replied Nick, demonstrating with him hands how he pushed Paul.

"That's all, for now, Mr Freeman. As I said, we are just trying to piece together Mr. Robertson's life and death."

"You have got to see it from their point of view, Caroline," said Angela, thoughtfully, as she could see that her friend hadn't slept the previous night.

"What are you saying. You really think that Nick is guilty. I can't believe this. You keep implying that Nick did this. Why? How can you be a true friend. If I need your help, and I can't see I will, I will let you know. Bye, Angela."

Caroline has now cut herself off from the rest of the village. She takes her girls to and from school, ignoring the playground gossips. She ignores Angela's phone calls and hides behind the curtains when she visits. She must just concentrate on Nick and the children, now. The police presence has dwindled, and everyone seems to have other subjects to talk about. Paul's murder remains a mystery.

Nick Freeman is the gentlest, non-aggressive man anyone could meet, thought Caroline, as she sat by herself after the girls had gone to bed. Nick was in his study She hadn't bothered to switch the lights on. The television remained on but, Caroline took no interest in the news. The bookmark in the library book was on the same page where she had left it the day before she discovered the body. Yes, she discovered the body. Why didn't she leave it? He may never have been found. He wouldn't have been missed. What are you thinking of, Caroline? He was a human being. When did you become so cruel?

Nick Freeman has always been quiet. In his own words, he was never one of the in crowd. He enjoyed school and worked hard. He had a few close friends who had shared the same interests. They would get together and fix things, experiment. Nick and his friends would combine their chemistry sets and mix chemicals, much to the fear of their mothers. Numbers also fascinated Nick. Is only interest in football was working out the points of the league tables. He didn't play football, rugby, cricket or any other team game. Although, he did now play cricket for Barker's End. It was more of a social, really. He wasn't any good. Nick's Dad and older brother were concerned that he would be a target for bullies, when he started secondary school. His mother's reaction was to leave the child alone. He would be all right. His Mum was right. He was never bullied. He was such a nice person.

When Nick got to into the University of this choice the family worried that he wouldn't make friends or cope away from home. He didn't make a lot of friends or attend parties. Too much alcohol made him feel out of control He was so interested in his chosen course that the social life didn't bother him. It was at University that he met the love of his life, Caroline. Caroline wasn't part of the in crowd, either.

Nick loved his job but, he loved his family a whole lot more. Caroline and his daughters were his world. He was a very happy man. Life in Barker's End had no downsides. He was popular in the village and nobody disliked him.

Caroline thought of Nick. He was a loving husband and a good father. He had told her that when he was growing up his father and tried to toughen him but, the toughening up had failed. He never went where fights were likely to break out. Night clubs were never his scene. This man, Caroline's husband, was no more capable of murder than Mother Teresa!

Caroline was settled, watching her favourite soap. This was something that she wouldn't have been able to concentrate on a few weeks before.

"I'll get it," shouted Nick as he was already on his way to open the front door.

"Hello, Inspector, sorry Chief Inspector, have you caught Paul's murderer? Nice of you to come and let us know. Tea. Coffee? Sit down."

"No sir, we haven't come to tell you that, unfortunately. We would like to ask you some questions, down at the police station."

"What. I told you everything when you were here before."

"I know you did Mr Freeman but, some evidence has been brought to our attention which links you to Mr. Robertson. We have a car outside, Sir."

Caroline could not believe what had just happened. She telephoned Angela who came to her friend's aid, immediately.

"Don't worry. You know that they can't solve this one, so they are clutching at straws. Nick was the last person to have a row with Paul. They won't be able to arrest him. They have nothing and, you know it. What is this new evidence, anyway?"

"They wouldn't say. What will happen to him? I know he didn't do it. Please stay here tonight with me, Angela. Will Chris mind? Why does everyone keep on about the argument with Paul. How does the whole village know this?

"Not, sure that I can answer all of the questions. I can say that Chris won't mind me staying here. I will just pop and get my toothbrush and let him know."

"Well, Mr. Freeman, as you know we removed some items from your garage. The rope that was used to strangle Mr. Robertson was the same type that we found on your premises. The forensic tests show that the fibres match those found on the body."

"No, Inspector, this can't be right. I have told you thousands of times that I didn't kill him." Nick was shocked and confused by the latest information. How could this be happening. "Perhaps someone borrowed the rope."

"Isn't that highly unlikely Mr. Freeman. You garage is very tidy and a meticulous man like yourself would know if anything had been touched."

Apart from the rope, the police had insufficient evidence to keep Nick in custody. The rope could have been used by someone else. There were quite a few sets of fingerprints in the garage. They couldn't hold him any longer.

"Caroline, I'm back but, before you get too relieved, I need to ask you something," Nick shouted as he came through the front door. "Has anyone been in the garage? Have the girls been playing in there? Did you leave the door open, by mistake?"

"What do you mean by all of this? I don't go into the garage. You use the car. Anyway, the car is never in the garage. What do I want in the garage? You don't think I am going to let the girls play in there. It's too dangerous with the tools and things. Oh, I did go in there the other week, I can't remember when. It was to get my wellingtons to dig over the bottom of the garden. I remember because Angela popped round and was laughing at how elegant there were, not."

"Angela, could she have touched anything?"

"Angela? She's hardly a rummaging in a garage type, is she?"

Nick told Caroline about the latest police questioning but, they couldn't solve the rope mystery. They knew that Nick wasn't completely in the clear. Not until they had found the real murderer.

James now had the perfect opportunity to have Caroline all to himself. Family life with the woman he had always loved would suit him well. He couldn't believe his luck when he was assigned to the case of the Barker's End murder. He was even more fortunate that Nick and the victim had had an argument. James had the means to set up his rival as a murderer. Life couldn't be better.

"It's James, isn't it? I thought it was you," Angela called out as she saw him on the garage forecourt.

"Yes, hello Angela."

"Caroline is my best friend and I know about you two. I may have a proposition for you but, I need to know the truth."

"What are you talking about. I've got to go. I'll be late."

"I care about Caroline. What about you? Is she just a fling or do you genuinely have feelings for her?"

"You're too late. Caroline has ended our relationship. She couldn't take any more stress."

"I think that you may be interested in what I have to say."

"Look, can we meet later. I can see that you are not a woman to be messed with. Meet me in the coffee shop, next the Newston Building Society, in town, on the High Street. I am not working today. Just give me an hour. See you there."

"What's all this about. I can understand that you care about your friend but, this is all a bit secretive."

"You haven't answered my question. My turn to be detective," Angela giggled.

"I do love Caroline. I wouldn't hurt her. I wouldn't even let Nick find out about us."

"When you say, love. You would look after her and the girls if she left Nick?"

"Yes. God, you are a good friend but, what is your plan? How can you help?"

"Caroline hasn't been happy with Nick for years. They don't show it, of course but, she doesn't like him working away all of the time. She would never leave him because he is a brilliant father, when he is at home.

The girls adore him. Caroline has a nice, settled life. She would never jeopardise that. Well, not until you came along. You see, I think that she really has fallen for you. I think that she would be happier with you than Nick but, she needs a push. She must know be sure that you are prepared to take on the girls."

"I still don't understand what the proposition is."

"Nick has been arrested on suspicion of murder. You can make sure that the evidence is against him. He goes to prison. They get divorced You are free to start a life with your little, ready made family."

"Yes, that would suit me but, what's in it for you."

"I do really want to see Caroline happy, and I know that you are the man she wants and needs."

"Whatever your plan is I don't want to know about."

"You won't have too."

Chapter 3

Paul lived in the nearby town of Newston. He rented a room in a house owned by a widow. This is all that the police could find out about him.

"Mr. Robertson is, sorry, was a smashing tenant. Very quiet, although he did like a drink, or two. He was no trouble. He never came home in the early hours drunk. Or, he never appeared to be, drunk I mean. He always paid his rent on time, not like some I've had here. He didn't tell me anything. Might have told the other tenants but, I never saw him speak to anyone. Never went out with friends, no lady friends. He always left here alone. He might have met someone, I suppose but, as I said he told me nothing. Who'd want to kill him? Terrible business."

"Thank you, Mrs. Harris, you've been very helpful."

Paul Robertson had moved to Newston about four years ago. Mrs Harris had obtained references for him from people who had employed him to work in the local area. She had a lot of local contacts and she trusted her friends. It seemed that Paul specifically came to Newston to work on a large housing estate in a nearby village. He was taken on for a trial period. He was so good at his job that nobody asked any questions. There was a shortage of builders with his skills.

Paul grew up in a small town about two hundred miles from Newston. He was brought up by his father as his mother had died giving birth to him. Paul did reasonably well at school but, was not as academically gifted, as was his friend, Andrew. When he found out that his best friend, his only friend, was going to the sixth form college and leaving him behind the loss of their close friendship affected him badly. He had always thought of Andrew as the brother he never had. Andrew's family were his family.

Andrew's Dad always asked Paul to help him with jobs around the house and garden.

"You're good at this, lad. I can see you having a great future as a builder or, a gardener. Anything, really, where you can use your hands and that skill for detail that you have. Our Andrew isn't good with his hands. He's got brains, though. You can't have everything." Andrew's Dad was always pleased with the work that Paul had done.

"I would like to be clever, like Andrew but, I enjoy building and fixing," replied Paul, happy to help his friend's family.

"Don't you fix things at home?"

"Not really. Dad never had the time to teach me. He can do things but, he pays tradesmen."

"Well, your Dad has had to be Mum, as well, all of your life. How come you know all this, then?"

"I just picked it up. I love woodwork and metalwork at school."

Andrew and his Mother were in the kitchen one evening, after Paul had gone home.

"Paul is a nice lad, and we love having him here for meals. He has lovely manners, and your Dad appreciates his help. Even your sister enjoys his company, even though she won't admit it," laughed Andrew's Mum.

"I can never understand why you never go to his home. Is his Dad ok?"

"Yes, I have met his Dad. He seems nice enough but, with just the two of them, well you know I think Paul finds it quiet and a bit awkward to have company. His Dad's at work all day and he doesn't want to give him extra meals to cook," replied Andrew, thoughtfully.

"Yes, you're right. Anyway, he is always welcome here."

"Thanks, Mum. I know we are opposites in many ways but, Paul and I are close."

Paul couldn't be happier than spending time with Andrew and his family. Even if Andrew was concentrating on his studies, Paul would still go to his house. He got on so well with Andrew's parents and sister. His own Dad had done his best but, everything at home was too formal, serious, that sort of thing, with just the two of them. How he wished he had a Mum and a sibling.

Andrew went to University and Paul suffered the loss as it were a bereavement. He had no other friends. He had been part of a gang at school but, they all went their separate ways and Paul wasn't the sort of person to keep in touch or, make new friends.

Paul started an apprenticeship at the local builders when he left school. He was particularly good at practical work. Building and fixing things was his only pleasure in life but, his life was about to change.

Paul had just had his twenty first birthday. There wasn't a party or drinks down the pub with the lads. His father did give him some money, had a cake made and invited a few distant relatives over for tea. Paul wasn't really interested in the celebration. It was just another day and he would rather have been working. A few days after his birthday he noticed that his father seemed more cheerful, singing in the mornings. Whistling when he got in from work.

"Paul, son, I'm bringing someone home for their tea tonight, after work. If you get in before me, lad, can you just make sure the place is tidy. I'll see to the tea."

"OK. It must be someone important. It's not a boss, is it?"

"You'll see, soon enough. See you later."

Paul was about to meet the mystery dinner guest.

"Come on in, love. Meet Paul. I've told you all about him, haven't I pet?"

"Paul, this is Elaine. Me and her have become very good friends over the past few months."

"Hello," was all Paul would say.

Paul knew what this meant. It had always been him and his Dad. With no Andrew around and no other friends he was alone in the world.

"Dad, I'm not very hungry and I have got to get something finished in the shed. See you later." Paul left the house without a word to Elaine and crept up to his bedroom before Elaine left. He had to face his father at the breakfast table.

"Lad, you were a bit rude to my friend last night. What's the matter with you?"

"I think we all know she is more than a friend, Dad. You just carry on. Don't mind me. I'm off to work now. I'll be moving out soon."

Paul started to drink heavily after his Dad and Elaine were married. His father grew increasingly angry with his son and threw him out of the house.

David Robertson had always done his best for his only child but, he couldn't provide a mother's love. He and Paul were not poor. David cooked good food every evening when he got home from his full-time job. Paul had decent clothes and an annual holiday by the sea. The house was clean, the laundry up to date. David Robertson was proud of how he coped. He taught Paul good manners and always helped with homework. He was a model father and house-husband but, he only had time or effort for the practical. Paul was never encouraged to bring friends home. Social skills were not a necessity for Paul to learn.

David had been an engineer at the local car factory since he left school. He had met Paul's mother, Maureen, at work. Maureen had worked in the typing pool and David had fancied her from the day she delivered some paperwork to his department. He was a good looking young man. His son had inherited his dark hair, brown eyes and muscular build. David couldn't believe his luck when Maureen said yes, she would come to the pictures on Friday. Maureen and David fell in love within weeks of meeting and were married within the year. They bought a two-bedroomed house and within months Maureen was pregnant. The couple couldn't be happier. David never knew what went wrong at Paul's birth. He didn't care. He just knew he had lost the love of his life. At first, he accepted help form both sets of grandparents but, the grief wouldn't leave him. He resented them living if Maureen was dead. Maureen's parents took care of Paul when David was at work but, he didn't want them in the house when he got home. He taught himself how to cook. He would do everything that Maureen could do in the house. He wouldn't let her down. Their child was going to be looked after. This was his duty to the memory of the only woman he had ever loved.

David never looked at another woman until he saw Elaine. Elaine worked in the accounts office. She was an attractive woman in her forties. Elaine delivered an invoice to his department supervisor, just as Maureen had done, all that time ago. David looked up from the engine he had been working on. Thinking back, did he only ask Elaine out because of the coincidence. Not many women had visited his department during the time that David had been employed at the factory. He knew Elaine was divorced. He had heard the gossip. Their first date wasn't to the cinema. They were middle-aged and sophisticated. The theatre and dinner was his treat. The dates become more frequent but, Paul never said more than hello to Elaine. David's biggest regret was that his son never approved of his new relationship. He had to think of his future happiness but, Paul was the son of the love of his life.

Paul's bitterness over his Dad's new relationship affected his work life.

"Hey, Robertson, why don't you come out with us. New club just opened. How about it, tonight?" The mouthy plumber shouted across the site to Paul.

"No thanks. Nightclubs are not really my idea of fun."

"Look lads, he speaks. Pretty girls not your scene, not your idea of fun. Perhaps you would prefer one of us. A bit of fun with a bloke, that's it." The men on the building site laughed and nudged each other. "Don't tell us that you don't like a drink. We've heard that you have one for breakfast."

Paul couldn't take it any longer. As his hammer flew into the air, narrowly missing the site foreman's head, the whole site fell silent. This was instant dismissal.

Paul had not only lost his home and the respect of his father, but he was also sacked by the builders. He loved that job but his behaviour on the site left his bosses no choice.

Paul had to get his drinking under control. He wasn't an alcoholic. He never drank during the day. He never had bottles of whiskey stashed behind the toilet cistern. He wasn't going to meetings. No, he could do this himself. He just had to find work. He would spend his life working, with the odd pint or two in the evenings. He liked work. He just wasn't one of the lads. A reference, for a new job, could be a problem, though.

Paul Robertson had left his childhood behind. His home life was not particularly happy with his father. After his father had re married and his adopted family life collapsed, he decided that he would always be better off alone.

Paul moved away after seeing an advert for builders on a new estate about two hundred miles away. He had nothing to lose. He couldn't believe his luck when he wasn't asked for references. The job had to be completed. He just had to prove himself. Paul never looked back. It was easy to get a job where nobody knew him. He was going to keep it that way. The whole country was desperate for skilled builders. He had no formal qualifications but, he was skilled.

Paul loved being alone with no ties. He had had a few girlfriends. He was very good looking and could be charming if he felt like it. The last thing he wanted was to be tied down. Why have children to worry about?

Why be home every evening at six for dinner. All that shopping and home decorating. It wasn't for him. He had seen that a wife and family didn't always lead to happiness. He had made the right decision.

The houses were finished on schedule but, that meant Paul was out of work. He put an advert in the local newsagent's window and he soon had plenty of work. The village of Barker's End, near to the town had plenty of wealthy residents all wanting house extensions. Word of mouth meant that he was never out of work. He visited the pub and chatted to the local men but, he never got involved in their lives and none of them ever really liked him. The women of the village were really quite interested in Paul. He was good looking, and his moody personality attracted them to him. It was rumoured that Paul had many affairs with the local women but, nothing was proved.

Paul had been in love, once, in his teenage years. It was with Andrew's sister. It probably wasn't real love, he had often told himself. She was the only girl he knew. The other girls at school ignored him, much the same as the boys, really. He did tend to attach himself to gangs but, nobody was really interested in him. He wasn't bullied, physically or verbally. He was just there, and nobody cared except for Andrew. He loved Andrew's whole family set up and his sister was part of that. The breakdown of Andrew's family was as much a shock to him as to the real family members.

He had plenty of work and one day he had a shock, when he went to quote for a new extension on a house. He knew it was her as soon as she opened the door. He waited to see if she recognised him. He had no intention of revealing her past to anyone. What had he to gain?

She was, after all, his first love. His first experience of girls. His only love, so far. He was in the village to work. He wasn't a gossip. He had no one he wanted to gossip to. Her secret was safe with him.

Paul was happy with life. Work was plentiful. He never had dreams of marrying and having a family. Family life wasn't all it was cracked up to be. He grew up with just a father and the only family that he felt part of had let him down in the end.

Paul despised the women of the village. He could have gone to bed with most of them he worked for. They were rich, bored housewives and he was wanted as their past time. He would never go to bed with her. It wasn't that he didn't fancy her. He respected her too much. There was one that he did quite fancy but, their relationship was platonic. He knew, she was like the rest of them, wouldn't leave her husband. He did buy her the occasional gift. Why? He didn't know. It wasn't like him.

Paul did start a relationship with a Barker's End resident. He couldn't believe his luck when his feelings were reciprocated. They had no plans to marry but, their relationship had become serious. Paul was happy that they had made plans to live together. They wouldn't live local. There would be too much scandal. He would never work locally, again. This didn't bother Paul. He could work in any part of the country, probably the world. He had no ties. He had finally found the real love of his life.

He wasn't interested in the women of the village but, he knew that a young, decent woman, with two little girls was having an affair, and he didn't approve.

"Hello, Mrs Freeman. I don't think that we have met before. I'm Paul."

"Hello, we haven't met before but, I have heard all about your building skills," replied Caroline, a little bemused as to why the local builder had introduced himself. "We don't need any work doing, if you are touting for business," she laughed, nervously.

"No, I am not here in connection with building work but, you could say I'm here on business so, perhaps, we could come to a business agreement."

"Whatever do you mean? Is it my husband you need to see? Do you want him to do your accounts?"

"No, Mrs Freeman, it's you that I think I could do business with."

Caroline was scared. She had heard everything about this man. Angela and, other Mums had said he was a very good builder. She had also heard that he provided services to the ladies of the village, which did not involve a hammer and nails or, so she assumed. Nick knew him, vaguely, from the pub. He wasn't a very popular with the other men. Perhaps they knew what was going on between him and their wives but, couldn't prove it. Caroline required neither a builder nor sexual favours. What did he want?

"Could we discuss this in private? I promise that this will be to your advantage."

Caroline was really scared, now, and didn't know what to do.

"Could we meet in the new café, in Newston High Street, The Teapot?" Caroline tried to sound composed. She wanted to meet this stranger in a public place.

"Yes, fine by me. You pick a date and time. See you soon, Mrs Freeman."

Caroline didn't want to meet Paul but, her curiosity outweighed her feelings of fear, well at the moment, anyway. What was going to happen to her in the café. It was a popular new venue. It would be full of customers. She wouldn't even mention this to Angela until she had found out more. She had asked Paul if he was free the next day. She knew she was in for a sleepless night so, better to get it over with.

It's was precisely 9.30am and Paul sat, sipping his drink, on a seat by the window. Oh no, she thought, everyone will see us here. She would have to say that they were discussing a new extension on her home. Why in the café? This wouldn't satisfy the gossips. You would discuss this in your home, with the builder measuring up, tutting and giving you an account of all the problems in your home. This excuse will have to do. I can't think of the neighbours at the moment.

"Hello, Mrs Freeman."

"Please call me Caroline."

"Well, Caroline. I will get straight to the point," Paul lowered his voice as he leant across the table towards Caroline. "What is it worth for me to keep quiet about your little secret with the local copper? The young man that visits you when your husband is away."

"Pardon, I don't know what you are talking about," Caroline was trying to be quieter despite her hysteria.

"Come along, Mrs Freeman. I am sure that Mr Freeman is not aware of the local Policeman's friendly visits," mocked Paul.

"You must be getting me muddled up with one of the women you see."

"What woman might that be, Mrs Freeman?"

"I don't know. Can we talk about your fantasies somewhere quieter?"

"Ah, you want to hear more then. Perhaps your place would be better for us to continue our chat."

Caroline left the café and headed for home. Paul had arrived ahead of her, in his van.

That's strange, thought Angela, as she passed Caroline's house. She didn't tell me that she was having some work done.

"Mrs. Freeman, it is best that you just admit it and we can come to some financial arrangement so, this won't go any further."

What could she do? She was trapped. She couldn't let Nick find out about her and James. Surely, Angela wouldn't have told anyone. For the sake of her daughters and her marriage she would have to dip into her savings and pay Paul the agreed amount.

"Can I ask you how you found out and, how you knew that he was in the police force?"

"It wasn't difficult. I have been working on the house next door. You know, the new couple; just moved in. I knew the young copper, in question. He had visited me when I had had some tools stolen from my van. I also knew that he wasn't Mr Freeman, as I'd heard him chat in the pub. I learn a lot by keeping my mouth shut. I couldn't make it out that he seemed to visit you when you were completely alone. You made some serious mistakes with your boyfriend. When I am up the ladder, working on the window frames, next door, I can see everything in your bedroom. Yes, you did always draw the curtains but, you had entered the room together. You don't want to make those kinds of mistakes if you are having an affair, Mrs. Freeman. It just leaves me to give you my address. You can drop the first instalment of cash off, in an envelope, through the letter box.

Mrs. Harris, my landlady, thinks the world of me and knows that I receive a lot of payments in cash. Even if she guesses that the envelope is full of cash, she will know that it is for work. Although, you must understand I do keep good records all Vat and tax paid on my cash sales. I'm not a tax evader, Mrs Freeman. Of course, I won't be able to account for our little bit of business," Paul chuckled as he spoke. "Mrs Harris is completely trustworthy. Oh, your nosey friend will want to know why I am here. Just tell her the neighbours were having a delivery so, I had to use your driveway. They are a nice couple. They don't know anyone in the village, yet."

As Paul started up his van Caroline did not know how she had got herself into this mess. This doesn't happen to people like me. Not me. She sobbed and automatically reached for the bottle of wine in the fridge.

"Only me," Angela cheerily greeted Caroline as she entered the hallway, after Caroline had, reluctantly, opened the front door. "Was that Paul's van outside?"

"Oh yes, he's doing some work next door for the couple next door that have just moved in. I don't think that you have met them, yet? Please say that you haven't got your claws into the newcomers, already," Caroline tried to sound as bright as her friend.

"No, I'm sure we will meet soon. Anyway, do you and Nick want to come over for lunch on Sunday? Are you ok?"

"Yes, that will be lovely. I think that I am getting a cold, that's all."

"As long as you are fit by Sunday. See you tomorrow for our walk."

"Yes, see you after the school run, bye."

Another glass of wine, then I will have to sort out the house. What am I going to do? Just pay up, Caroline. It won't stop, though. Blackmailers don't just ask for a one-off payment. Maybe he will. I will just have to wait and see. Who's that at the door, now?

"Oh, it's you. No, you can't come in. I can't see you again."

"What's up with you? Why are you drinking, during the day, on your own? Caroline?" said James, as he could see the glass on the kitchen table.

"Just go. I can't see you ever again."

"What's wrong? Does Nick know about us?"

"No but, someone else does. That's all I am saying. Just go."

"Who?"

"Just go, please go," Caroline was hysterical as she slammed the door.

James walked to his car, confused by Caroline's outburst. He recognised the attractive woman who was crossing the road.

"Angela?"

"James," how can I help you?"

James told Angela that, as far as he knew, she was the only one who knew about his relationship with Caroline. Did Angela know why she wanted to end their affair?

"You didn't have anything to do with her decision, did you?" he asked Angela, accusingly.

"I didn't know that she didn't want to see you again but, I think it's a good idea. Caroline is a happily married Mum, and she is not cut out for this sort of life."

"That is not what you said, last time we met. You encouraged our relationship. Have you threatened to tell Nick?"

"No, of course not, she's my friend and, although I don't approve of her affair and I approve even less of you, I wouldn't betray her trust. I care about her whereas, with you is all about sex."

"For your information I do actually love her. I just think that she is afraid that someone is going to tell Nick."

"Well, it will never be me."

"Sorry, I think that we both want to protect her. Thank you. Goodbye Angela."

Angela had been confused about her conversation with James. Who knew about the affair?

"Hello, back so soon? come in. I've just heard from Nick. He is going to be late, again, tonight. Wine?"

"Caroline, I have just had a conversation with your lover. He accused me of letting the cat out of the bag. Caroline, are you drinking a bit too much, lately?"

"Angela, how could you say that? I couldn't keep up with you."

"No, I know but, it's not like you."

Caroline had enjoyed her arrangement with James. It stops her life being dull. Neighbours and friends would never suspect that mousey, prim little Caroline could possibly be having an affair. Angela, the only person who Caroline has told of her double life, would be the ideal candidate for an affair. Flirty, loud and extravert. Everything that Caroline isn't. Caroline is never going to leave Nick. She enjoys her cosy life and would never hurt Nick or jeopardise her daughter's happiness. She trusts Angela to keep her secret and has no reason to believe that anyone will ever find out. She had ended the affair but, it was too late.

James had found out that Paul Robertson knew of his affair with Caroline. Paul had often seen James's car parked outside of her house. Although Paul didn't mix socially with the locals, he spent a lot of time in the village, working on various houses. He knew who was invited to who's dinner party, what mother was worried about her child's spelling, who was sleeping with who. Paul knew it all. He listened to telephone conversations, heard the gossip from the coffee and wine gatherings and knew who was visiting who. Paul never had conversations with his customers that were not work related. As far as they were concerned he was the builder. He is sullen, moody but, a good workman. This is just what Paul wants. This image is all part of the plan. Paul sees James as an easy target. James would do anything to keep his career.

"James isn't it?" Paul stepped out of his van as the police detective was crossing the road.

"Who wants to know?" replied James, although he had an idea of who it was that was taking a sudden interest in him.

"I'm Paul Robertson. I don't think that we have met. I won't keep you long, James. I can call you James or, would you prefer Sergeant Watson? I want to talk to you about a financial arrangement. Perhaps it would be better if we could sit in your car."

"I can't see any reason to discuss finances with you. You're a builder. That's right, isn't it?"

"I think that you might like to hear what I have to say. Your car would be so much more comfortable than my dirty van, full of tools. You don't want to mess up that smart suit."

James unlocked the car and Paul got into the passenger seat.

"You see, James. I know that you and Mrs Freeman see quite a lot of each other. And I do mean a lot of each other, literally."

"Yes, Robertson. I know where this is leading. Caroline did tell me that you are blackmailing her so, now you are trying your luck with me. I've not got a marriage to save, so it won't work on me."

"No, but you do have a career that I believe you are very keen to progress in."

"I am fond of my job and good at it. There is nothing in the police rule book to say that a policeman cannot have an affair with a married woman."

"No, James, I am sure that is correct but, I am sure that some of the time you were with Mrs Freeman, you were supposed to be on duty. Is that true, James?"

"You have no way of proving anything."

"I haven't, but would you want to take that risk?"

"You are wasting your time. Caroline has ended our affair."

"That may be the case but, she has admitted it did happen so, I'm sure that you would want to cooperate."

Blackmail wasn't an easy crime for Paul to commit. He wasn't a completely innocent person. He had had his skirmishes in the past but, this was out of his league. It served them right. Caroline was risking her family's happiness. Those little girls would have their lives ruined. That young copper will want to keep his job as much as Caroline will want to keep her family. Blackmail isn't nice but, neither is what they are doing. The money won't go to waste. I know just what I am going to do with it.

Chapter 4

Hilary Patterson, in Caroline's opinion, has always thought that she was better than anyone else.

"Hello, Caroline. We really must meet for coffee, one day. My place, of course," shouted Hilary across the Playground.

"Yes, we must," was Caroline's softly spoken response.

That's never going to happen, mumbled Caroline, to herself, through gritted teeth. She is only inviting me so that she can gleam the information about the murder from me. She must love the fact that Nick had been arrested.

Hilary had married into a wealthy family. Her husband, Marcus, had a good job as an architect for the local council. Angela and Chris were always invited to Hilary and Marcus's many dinner parties but, Caroline and Nick were not. Caroline is convinced that Nick would have been invited if he had a more acceptable partner but, she knew she couldn't compete with the Hilarys and Angelas of this world. Angela was a loyal friend but, the same could not be said of Hilary.

The village residents assumed that Hilary's family were always rich but, no one knew anything about Hilary's past, not even Marcus.

Hilary Patterson was born in a small town about two hundred miles from Barker's End. Life couldn't be happier for Hilary. Many of her school friends were going through the rebellious, moody, early teenage years. Hilary saw this as an affliction. Her best friend, Gillian, had agreed it was a very accurate description and they were proud that they knew such a grown up word and didn't suffer with this affliction. The girls grew up on the same street and both shared an enthusiastic love of life. They both came from loving, stable families. Hilary had no interest in dating boys, yet. She was rather fond of her brother's friend but, he was more like an extra brother and she appreciated the friendship and care that they both showed her. Her parents, especially her Dad, were relieved that her only interest in the opposite sex was with popstars. She spent a lot of time in her room listening to music and drooling, as her mother would say, over some good looking singer. She never spent money on make-up. Why should she with her big blue eyes, perfect white teeth and flawless complexion. She loved clothes and would spend time and money, that she received for Christmas and her birthday, buying the latest top, trousers or shoes. Gillian always accompanied her on these shopping expeditions. Hilary was popular with her peers because she was never miserable or moody. She had no reason to be.

Hilary's father worked in the local factory as a supervisor and her mother was a housewife. Hilary wasn't as clever as her brother but, was hard working at school.

Hilary and Gillian had gone into town to spend her birthday gift voucher.

"Are you going to get this gorgeous, pink top?" asked Gillian. "You will still have some money left over for underwear. I wish I had such generous relatives," sighed Gillian.

"Yes, I might get the top but, just one more look around. I haven't looked at everything, yet."

"Oh, Hilary, you are always like this. You can never make up your mind. We must be home for tea in an hour. You know what the buses are like. Gillian was looking out of the shop window to relieve the boredom, while her friend made up her mind.

"Come here, look. Is that your Mum getting into that car? Come, quick, to the window. Is that your uncle she is with? My uncles don't look like that. None of them."

"Yes, it is her. That's my Uncle Frank. I don't think that you have met him. Gillian, I have gone off this top. We could just catch the number 6 if we hurry," said Hilary putting the garment back on the hanger.

"You're not spending the voucher, then? You don't want anything else?" questioned Gillian.

"No, I think we should just go."

"OK then, another day," replied Gillian, puzzled by her friend's sudden change of mood.

"Your Mum knows that we are in town, so she won't worry."

"Please let's just catch the bus," pleaded Hilary.

The friends didn't speak on the bus journey home. Gillian knew that something was wrong.

"See you at school, tomorrow, bye," said Hilary as she reached the gate.

"Yes, see you," said Gillian, walking slowly to her house as she thought about her friend's strange behaviour.

"Hello, good shopping trip?" asked Gillian's Mum as she heard her daughter enter the front door.

"Not really. Hilary's acting a bit weird."

"What do you mean, a bit weird. What sort of weird? Is she ill?"

"I don't think so."

"She'll be fine tomorrow. Just you wait and see. Teas nearly ready."

A few doors away, in the residential street, Hilary's mother greeted her daughter with a smile and a cup of tea when she entered the kitchen.

"What did you buy, then?"

"Oh, nothing. Couldn't find anything. Do you mind if I don't have any tea? I don't feel hungry."

"I hope you are not coming down with something. A lot of colds going around."

"Could be. I'm going to bed early."

Hilary went to her room but, couldn't sleep. The events of the last couple of hours were on her mind. She had seen that man before. The man who her mother was in town with. One day, when she had arrived at home early from school, the same man was just leaving her house. Her mother had told her he was her new insurance man. Her mother was blushing as she spoke and soon changed the subject. The insurance office was in town. Perhaps Mum had gone with him to sign something. That's it. What was I thinking? Despite her justifying the situation Hilary still didn't sleep at all. In the morning she really did feel ill and told her mother that she wasn't going to school.

"Oh, you'll be all right when you get there. I'm busy today and I can't stay and look after you." Her mother sounded rather agitated.

"You don't need to look after me. I'm thirteen. I'll just stay on the settee all day."

"No, no, you can't. Not today."

"Why not?"

Hilary insisted that she wasn't going to school. She phoned Gillian to say that she wouldn't meet her at the top of the road. At least Gillian now had an explanation for her friend's behaviour. Hilary went to bed but, could hear her mother on the phone. She was obviously cancelling her arrangements.

A day later and Hilary was back to normal. She arranged with Gillian to go into town after school and spend her gift voucher.

"Are you going to buy something today? Are you really going to make up your mind?" laughed Gillian as they headed for the boutique.

"Yes, I think I still want that top, if it's still there."

Hilary did spend her voucher but, as they headed to the bus stop she said,

"Does Martins insurance company still have an office here?"

"I don't know. Why?" replied a puzzled Gillian.

The two girls looked for the office and asked passers by but, no one knew of Martins office.

"What do you need insurance for? We're a bit young to be thinking of that sort of thing. Shopping for gorgeous tops is more our scene," laughed Gillian.

"No, just, nothing, really."

The girls walked from the bus stop and Gillian thought that her friend's mood had changed, again. Perhaps she hadn't had enough time off school to get over her virus.

The months went by and everything seemed normal at home and school. Hilary's brother was still bringing his best friend home and then disappearing upstairs to play the latest record. The happy household was the same. Dad making his daft jokes when he came in from work. Mum cooking and cleaning and always looking glamourous for a housewife but, that was Mum.

Gillian and Hilary are still the best of friends and spend most of their free time together but, Gillian is about to ruin her friend's happiness.

"Hilary, I meant to tell you. I saw your Mum with your Uncle Frank the other afternoon. I'd gone into town with my Mum. You know the day we left school early because the heating went off," said Gillian, as they walked to school.

"Did she see you? Did she speak?"

"No, I think she and your uncle were too busy laughing. Is he her brother?"

"Yes, yes he is."

Hilary was convinced now that her mother and the insurance man, if that's what he really was, were having an affair. Her mother had always been attractive. There were no signs of an affair. What are the signs? She would tell her brother. He would know what to do. He was clever.

"Don't be stupid. This is some girlie, romantic idea. You read those silly girl's comics. This is our Mum you're talking about. Don't let Dad hear your daft talk."

"No, Andrew, listen, it's true. He's been to the house. We've seen them in the car."

"What you and Gillian? She's as daft as you with her giggling and whispering. Why don't we just ask Mum."

"No, we can't. She'll deny it. Should we tell Dad?"

"Yes, we will tell Dad. He will say what I said to you. He will make one of his daft jokes. You know Dad."

They did tell their father and, he already had his suspicions.

Hilary's father moved out of the house. Hilary and her big brother met him every weekend in town. They were both too old to have the treats and outings that come with an absent father. They just went to cafes. Their Dad would not let them see the bed-sit he lived in. He was too ashamed. Hilary loved her Dad so much and hated her mother for breaking up the family. Gillian was a great support and Hilary became part of her friend's family and spent as much time with them as she could. Her home was just for bed and breakfast.

Her brother spent more time with his best friend and Hilary thought of him as another brother. Someone she could rely on.

When Hilary was at home she noticed that her mother was drinking. This wasn't anything that had happened in their household. Drinks were for Christmas. A glass of sherry from a bottle that lasted until the next year. Brandy for shock. Uncle Frank was no longer interested, and the affair had ended. He had convinced his wife that the affair hadn't happened. Andrew, with the help of his friend, did try to help his mother, as he felt sorry for her and wasn't as bitter towards her as Hilary was.

Andrew went to sixth form college and made new friends. He couldn't hide his excitement when he gained a place at Cambridge University. Hilary realised that his support for her and his mother was now in the past. His best friend was no longer in touch. This was a new life for him. Hilary wasn't old enough to leave home and her love and respect for her big brother had now turned to anger.

Hilary had to wait until she left school before she could move away. She wasn't old enough to live alone but, she could go and live with her Aunt and Uncle. Gillian had a steady boyfriend so, there was nothing to keep her in her home town. She spent her spare time writing for office jobs which she found in the newspaper that her Aunt had sent her every week. She was still upset by her family's breakdown but, looked to her new life. Her Auntie and Uncle were great landlords. They never had children of their own so, treated her as a grown up.

Hilary made up her mind that the route to success in life was to work hard. The girls at work were friendly and her social life was good. She went out on a few dates but, studying for her business studies exams was her priority. The company she worked for was a family business. Her bosses, Mr. and Mrs. Patterson, liked to reward hard work and she was promoted to Office Manager within two years. She was still only twenty and work meant a lot more to her than a husband and family. She thought of her past and couldn't see the advantage to family life. It could all go wrong.

The Christmas party was, for the first time, going to be held at the Patterson's home. They certainly had the room. Hilary arrived with some of her colleagues and thought she was entering a stately home.

"Wow," they said in unison when the taxi stopped at the top of the gravel drive.

Hilary nervously entered the hallway. She had met everyone before but, this was different. In the hallway stood the most handsome man she had ever seen. Marcus Patterson saw her as she was removing her coat.

"Hello, let me get you a drink. I'm Marcus. You haven't seen me at work because I won't work for them," he chuckled. "I'm their son," he stared at Hilary as he held out his hand. "I'm a great disappointment to them as I won't take over the family business and am studying to be an architect."

"Pleased, to meet you. I'm Hilary and I am sure they are very proud of you," said Hilary, wondering if she should have said anything.

"You're the one that my parents have high hopes for. In their eyes you can do no wrong. Hard working, helpful, intelligent and, now I can see, beautiful as well."

"Now, I'm really embarrassed and have got a lot to live up to."

"Anyway, that drink?" reminded Marcus.

"Just a coke please, I don't drink."

Hilary had never drank alcohol since witnessing the effect it had on her mother.

"Coke it is, then. Let's find a quiet corner and I can get to know you."

Marcus and Hilary enjoyed many dates before they announced their engagement to his parents and her Aunt and Uncle. Hilary had pleaded with her Aunt and Uncle not to ever say where she was really from and what had happened to her real parents. She had no idea if they were dead or alive and she never saw Andrew again after he went to Cambridge. Andrew never forgave her for leaving their mother when she needed help. Hilary would argue that it was his responsibility too but, it was alright for him with his posh, new life. Their father suffered from depression after the separation from their mother and he lost his job.

In Hilary's mind she was an orphan. Her Aunt and Uncle were happy to go along with the story because Hilary was the daughter they had never had. They were heartbroken at the break-up of Hilary's parent's marriage but, they too had lost contact with them.

Hilary and Marcus were married and held the reception at the Patterson family home. Uncle Phil was as proud as any father when he gave Hilary away. Aunt Mary was glamourous in her mother of the bride outfit. Hilary couldn't be happier but, she did have a moment of sadness when she thought how lovely her real mother would have looked on this day. Marcus's parents were delighted with their son's choice of wife and Hilary knew that her promotion had nothing to do with her falling for the boss's son. She was going places at it would all be her own merit.

Marcus was doing well in his career as an architect and was offered a job working for a local authority planning office. It meant moving away. They had already bought a house close to his parent's home and Hilary continued to work for the family business. Marcus could not turn down the offer of the job so, the couple had to move away. Hilary would never have to work again if, she chose not to.

Hilary had settled into village life in Barker's End and announced her pregnancy soon after they moved. Although she had ideas of furthering her career, she found the idea of being a housewife and mother even more appealing. She did continue working from home, for the Patterson's. She knew they would never need the extra money and, for the first time in her life a lady who lunched lifestyle was beckoning. Yes, things were going to change. She would be moving in different circles. The impending fatherhood caused Marcus to question his wife about her family.

"You said yourself that you were eighteen when you moved in with Mary and Phil. You weren't a child, Hilary. Tell me about your Mum and Dad."

"I had a breakdown just before I moved in with Auntie. This caused me to lose my memory. The doctors said it was the shock of losing my Mum and Dad. I know nothing about their deaths. Mary and Phil wouldn't tell me. They were afraid it would be too traumatic for me. They tell me I was an only child." Hilary had rehearsed this lie many a time and her Aunt and Uncle agreed to her wishes. This version of events did seem to satisfy Marcus and he told her how lucky she was to have Mary and Phil.

Hilary gave birth to Robert, named after Marcus's father. A perfect baby for the couple's perfect lifestyle. Robert was so well behaved that they could carry on giving the best dinner parties in the village and the baby would sleep through the evenings. Hilary became a perfect snob, much to Marcus's irritation. Her in-laws were not impressed by her new image. Despite their wealth, and business success, they were a very down to earth couple and they had admired this in their former employee and daughter-in-law. Hilary, herself, couldn't explain this change of character. She knew that her life was perfect. She felt that she had made it. Why shouldn't she feel superior after such traumatic teenage years.

Two years after Robert's birth. Mary, his baby sister was born. Marcus insisted that his daughter be named after the Aunt that had done so much for his wife. Hilary agreed to the name but, no longer saw much of her Aunt and Uncle and she now thought that they were beneath her.

"I think that we need an extension," Hilary announced one day.

"Why?" replied Marcus peeping over the top of his newspaper.

"The children need a playroom. We could have a proper dining room. It's awful having to eat at one end of the lounge when we have guests."

"Well, we could afford it and I don't see us moving away from here."

"Good, glad you agree. Should I get some quotes?"

"I'll see a couple builders we deal with but, there is one who works in the village. The pub lads say he does a good job. He's a bit grumpy but, excellent worker."

"Send them all round. We can choose the best quote," said Hilary, excited by the new project. "I will, of course, manage the work myself."

"I thought you would, somehow," said Marcus, rather sarcastically.

"The sooner we get this done, the better. I will cancel my meeting with the girls if you can send the builder you know round tomorrow."

"The two you sent round today were nice chaps. I don't mind which one we have."

"Let's wait for the quotes in writing. We still have Paul. He is coming round tomorrow. You will be here, yes?"

"Yes. Is that the Paul who does a lot of work in the village? I've heard he is a bit rough. Not much personality, either."

"Yes, that's him but, if he is a good a builder as they say he is and, the price is right, who cares about his social skills."

Hilary waited, in anticipation, for this supposedly fantastic builder.

"Hello, I'm Paul Robertson. I've come to quote you for some building work."

"Please come in and I'll show you what needs doing. I know my husband has done proper plans. That's his job, you know."

Paul didn't speak. He just made notes and took measurements, whilst studying the plans.

"He looked familiar," said Hilary as she poured Marcus a drink.

"Who did?"

"The builder who came here, today. He might look like someone famous. It will come to me soon."

The quotes arrived by post, except Paul's, who delivered his by hand.

"Paul Robertson is the best and, he does come highly recommended. I think we'll go with him."

"I'll phone him tomorrow," shouted Hilary from the kitchen.

My God. I know who he is. It can't be. Hilary was sipping her second cup of tea after Marcus had left for work. Paul Robertson; same name. Did he remember me? Is it really him? I must do some digging. I'll ring the girls and find out what they know about him. If it is him, we can't let him work here. Does he live in the village? How can I convince Marcus to hire one of the other builders? Calm down. Paul Robertson is a common name. He would have said if he had remembered you. You were on your own so, he had no reason not to say anything. I'll invite the girls round for lunch, today. Wine for them. I must loosen their tongues and find out as much as I can about Paul.

"Hi, it's Hilary, why don't you come here today, for lunch? I know it's short notice but, I'm free today and I need some advice. I will telephone the others. Oh, can you ring everyone, on my behalf. Good, glad you can come. Don't bring anything. Just yourselves. Hello Fran. Please come to lunch today. I am just going to ring Marie and Angela. Oh, I suppose that Caroline will have to come if Angela comes. I have no idea why Angela hangs around with that little mouse. Oh, lovely to see you all. Caroline not with you, Angie? What a shame." Thank God was Hilary's reply through gritted teeth. "Wine everyone? Of course. Diets are suspended today. Food won't be long but, I need answers."

"What do you mean?" asked a puzzled Angela.

"I need to know about Paul Robertson, the builder."

"What about him. He is incredibly good. Is he doing your extension?" asked Ruth.

"Well, everyone says he's good but, he may be a mad axeman. Nobody knows anything about him but, you must have heard something. He has worked for some of you. Does he chat when you make him a cup of tea? Where does he live. Is he married?"

"No, he doesn't come from around here. He doesn't have a recognisable accent. No, we don't know anything. Sorry," Marie spoke and looked around the room for support from her friends.

"Well, does he have references?" asked Hilary, impatiently.

"No, just word of mouth. He is good."

"Lunch is served, ladies."

The lunch went well, and everyone went home a little tipsy. All very well, thought Hilary but, I still have no information about Paul. There is another possibility but, it's a risk and I still may not find the answers. Andrew. I must be careful to cover my tracks if I can't find out where Andrew went after Cambridge. I know what college he studied at but, will they tell me what he did. Will they know? Has he moved? This will all have to be done by telephone from the call box in the village. How can I put the extension off? Marcus knows I am keen to get it finished.

"Marcus, I know that this will surprise but, can we put the building work off for a little while?"

"Put it off, why? Are you ok?"

"Yes, it's just that the school holidays are in a couple of weeks. The children will be in the way I wasn't really thinking. It won't be very practical. Also, I have a lot of work to do for your Mum and Dad."

"Yes, I was thinking about that. Are you sure that it is not too much, to work for them, now that you have the children?"

"No, I have been doing this for years. You know that they couldn't do without me. You never said all this when they were little and at home all day. No, it gets easier, now that they at school. Anyway, I can't spend all my life socialising with the girls."

"Well, if you say so, Project Manager. We might miss out on Paul, though, the whole village wants his services."

"Never mind. We will have to take that risk," said a relieved Hilary. She has to put her plan into action.

Hilary walked furtively to the telephone kiosk on the High Street. If anyone sees me I will say my telephone is out of order. I can't make outgoing calls. She had worked it all out in her head.

"Hello, you don't know me but, I need to get in touch with Andrew Masters. It's very urgent."

"We have more than one Andrew Masters here, at the moment, madam. You will have to give m more details."

"Oh no, he is not at college, now. He graduated a few years ago, I think."

"I can't help you, madam. I can't give out information on previous students, even if I have that information to give."

"I realise that but, this is a family emergency."

"Well, if it's family, why don't you know where he is?"

Hilary put the receiver down. This is pointless. I will ask Paul if he knows Andrew. I won't say I am Andrew's sister. If he doesn't know Andrew, then it's not the Paul I know and everything is fine. Even if he knows Andrew, I will make up some story that I knew an Andrew when we were studying. He may not remember me.

"Marcus let's go ahead with the extension. The girls will take it in turns to have the children."

"Well, a woman's prerogative, I suppose, you know, to change her mind."

Hilary paced up and down, awaiting the arrival of the builder. There was something on her mind. Something made her feel uneasy.

"Hello, do come in. Do you want tea, coffee, before you start?"

"No thanks, no drink I like to just get started."

They were right about him being grumpy. Paul had his break and poured his tea from the flask. I know her from somewhere, he thought. Perhaps she looks like someone off the telly. It will come to me soon.

The extension was almost finished. Two rooms. A playroom and a dining room. Paul really was a good worker. He turned up early and worked late. He didn't chat but, that got the work done quicker. Hilary was fussy but, she couldn't find fault with either of the rooms.

Hilary never found the courage to mention Andrew but, one day her fears were realised. Paul was decorating the rooms himself. He had almost finished when one day, unusually, he spoke to Hilary.

"How are you, Hilary? You look like you have done well for yourself."

"I'm sorry, what do you mean."

"It's taken me months to remember how I knew you. The other night it came to me. All those years ago, Andrew's sister. I couldn't believe it."

"You must be mistaken. I haven't got a brother. I'm an only child. I must look like someone else called Hilary. There are a few of us around. You've just got the wrong Hilary."

Hilary remained composed, although she knew that this was the end of her cosy lifestyle. The worst that could happen has happened. Her past had caught up with her.

"After I realised who you were, I searched for a photo of the three of us. I knew I had one in an old case. I've got it here, today. I thought I would show you when I finish."

"No, that's not me. Who's that boy, anyway?"

"Hilary, I think you know that's you and your brother Andrew. Don't you see him anymore? I lost touch with him. We were good mates but, he was always clever. I couldn't mix with his sort. I was always good with my hands. Hilary, you used to be so close, such a happy family. Why don't you see Andrew?"

Hilary started to cry. She couldn't pretend anymore.

"My husband doesn't know about my past. I went to live with my Aunt and Uncle to get as far away from home as possible. I was lucky to get a good job and Marcus was the bosses son. Andrew thought that I could look after Mum while he was away at University. I was resentful of his freedom. I couldn't cope with Mum. You know it all went wrong. Don't try and blackmail me. Don't think that you can increase your charge," Hilary was defiant through her sobs.

"What do you take me for? I have built up a good little business round here. I don't want to blackmail you. I was enquiring about your welfare. You and Andrew were always good to me."

"Sorry, Paul. It's just that nobody knows about my past. Marcus thinks my parents died when I was young and that my Aunt and Uncle brought me up. Anyway, you can talk. Nobody knows anything about you! Do you know where Andrew is or, what happened to my parents?"

"Can't help you with your family. After I lost contact with you all I had a bit of bad luck, myself. I fell out with my Dad. If you remember there was just me and him after my Mum died giving birth to me. I didn't get on with my stepmother. Dad threw me out. I worked round the country doing odd jobs. I settled in Newston, near here. The work keeps coming. A lot of wealthy people round here, like yourself."

"Paul this can never come out. Marcus would probably leave me for telling so many lies. Please, you mustn't let anyone know. This is a small place."

"I have no reason to say anything. You know me but, you don't have to tell me about the gossips around here.

Just because I don't say much, I do listen," he laughed for the first time since they had known each other, probably since the whole village had known him. "I am sure Marcus wouldn't leave you. He may find out one day."

Hilary made herself a cup of tea after Paul had gone. She believed him. He had always been a good friend when they were young. He didn't convince her that the secret was safe. She had heard that he did get drunk in the local pub. He could become a bit more talkative, unintentionally.

Hilary couldn't risk her perfect lifestyle. How could she deal with Paul?

Marcus was a happily married. Or so he thought. Hilary could be a bit of a snob but, he would always love her. His children were brilliant, he didn't mean academically gifted. They were doing alright at school. He just meant that he loved them so much and they were reasonably behaved. He enjoyed his job, most of the time. Village life suited him so, life was good. He was feeling unsettled, yes that's the word, unsettled by this phone and that builder. He's not jealous, just puzzled by his wife's behaviour. He is a man who likes to sort out problems and let's look at the facts. Marcus was talking to himself when he should have been concentrating on work. He was ashamed to think that Hilary might have something to do with Robertson's murder. Of course, she is not a killer. Why did all these suspicions coincide with his death, though? Or around that time.

Marcus Patterson was surprised when Hilary didn't want Paul Robertson to work on the extension. She had seemed so eager to get it done. She had relented, in the end but, she still seemed nervous when Robertson was in the house. Marcus had heard the gossip that Paul was having affairs with every woman on the estate but, he wasn't having an affair with Hilary. He knew that because he was at home when some of the work was being done. The children were on school holidays for part of the time. Children can't keep secrets for long. They would have said something. The odd remarks at the dinner table. Why does Mummy send us round to next door's house when that builder man is here? Why did she tell us not to say anything to you, Daddy? You know what it's like. They mean to keep secrets but, can't.

Marcus was convinced that Hilary's strange behaviour wasn't to hide an affair. He wasn't sure that he believed the gossip, anyway. That Robertson bloke seemed too engrossed in his work to even notice women.

Why had Hilary got that pay as you go mobile? She had the latest Smart phone. He should know. She went on about having one for Christmas. She, probably, didn't know what to do with half of features on the phone but, she wasn't going to be left behind by her friends. She was going to have the latest technology. She didn't care if she didn't know how to use it.

Marcus wasn't checking up on Hilary when he discovered the mobile phone. It was on the floor, at the back of the wardrobe. Good plan, he thought to himself. Hilary knows that he wouldn't be vacuuming under the furniture. He just dropped his watch, one morning. He thought it had gone underneath the bed. He then discovered it, with the help of a torch, underneath the wardrobe. He used a coat hanger to retrieve the watch and something else moved towards the front of the cupboard. A phone. What for? Was it because she is having an affair? Who with? Is it that Robertson, after all? Marcus scrolls through the call history. Incoming and outgoing calls are all for the same area code. Let's have a look: Cambridge. Who do we know in Cambridge? How could Hilary be having an affair with someone that far away? Well, let's try ringing the numbers. A Cambridge college. Of course, that is what Cambridge is famous for. Why a college? The only connection I can think of is some of the blokes in the pub, that live here, did go to Cambridge University. Even if Hilary is having an affair with an ex-graduate, what would his college have to do with it? I will do some subtle digging down the pub. Let's try this other number. An incoming call comes from this as well. This one's a scientific company in Cambridge. None of the blokes up the pub work in that profession. Well, it could be a newcomer but, I can't see him travelling to and from Cambridge for work. More subtle digging. God, I'd forgotten. What about that time, Oh, who was it? He told me he didn't call about the golf on the landline, because Hilary was using a call box because the phone wasn't working. Well, that's what Hilary told his wife, when she saw her hurrying back from the phone box, down the High Street. Hilary never said that the phone was out of order. Perhaps she had one of those on-line checks and the problem was solved. Why was her call so urgent that she had to go to the call box? This must all be connected to the spare mobile. Well, I've made a note of these Cambridge numbers. I had better out this phone back where I found it. There is no point me asking her. She will deny everything. Make up some story. Yes, the pub is a good place to start.

"Keith, you know everything about everybody who drinks in here. Don't you?" asked Marcus.

"Not me, mate. You're confusing me with the wife. What do you want to know? I'll get her for you."

No hurry. I just need some advice. That's all." Keith went to fetch Kath, after the queue at the bar had died down.

"Hello Marcus. I hear that you want to know about something. Local is it?

"Not really but, it's work problem, really," Marcus lied. "I just need someone with a technical or scientific brain. I thought that you might know if one of your regulars has a science background. We're doing some work with a tech. firm, in Cambridge. You probably know someone who went to Cambridge. There are a lot of clever people around here. I just want a bit of background information, you know, a chat over a pint."

"Well, Marcus, a lot of your neighbours went to Cambridge University. Oh, it might be Oxford. A bit of both. It's all the same to me. There are all far too clever for the likes of me. I don't think any of them do that sort of work, though. I can't think that anyone would work in Cambridge and live here. You know that I can get information out of anyone, Marcus. You know me. I should have been a detective," giggled Kath as she pulled the pump to make sure Marcus's glass was filled to the top.

Marcus couldn't forget his findings. He had to find out what Hilary was so secretive about. He was fortunate that Kath was serving in the bar when he next went in for a drink.

"Just the man. Marcus, I did find something out. One of the regulars does have work, sometimes, in

Cambridge. Chris. Chris, you know. He's married to Angela. Everybody knows Angela."

Marcus did know Chris. He played cricket for the village, sometimes but, he was away a lot, for work. Marcus didn't know him that well. A nice chap, though. Hilary was a great friend of Angela's. The had met at Angela's dinner parties but, everyone was there. I'm sure Hilary is not having an affair with Chris.

Marcus started going out for a drink a lot more than he used too, much to Hilary's dismay.

"Hi, Chris, what are you having mate?"

"Marcus? Thanks, I'll just have a lager, please. It's hot out there, today. I always drink lager this weather," replied Chris, rather surprised that Marcus was offering him a drink. They didn't have much to do with each other.

"The truth is, I want to pick your brains."

I knew it, thought Chris to himself. He had never bought me a drink before but, a nice enough chap. I will help him if I can.

"I've heard that you have a client in Cambridge. Well, you do visit Cambridge."

"Well, yes I do but, I can't see how this can help you," a puzzled Chris put down his glass.

"Have you ever heard of Two Tech in Cambridge?"

"No, I can't say that I have but, the company that I am dealing with is not one of those High-Tech companies. What's this all about, anyway?"

"It's just that we may be working for them and just wondered if you knew anything about them. Just a long shot really. Enjoy your drink. See you around mate."

Chris was surprised when Marcus left, and he guessed that wasn't the real reason for their conversation.

He would ask Angela if Hilary knew about her husband's strange behaviour.

"What connections do Hilary and Marcus have with Cambridge?"

"What did you say, Chris?" Angela called from the kitchen as she was preparing another elaborate dinner.

Chris repeated the question but, Angela didn't know of any connections but, would try to find out. The next day Angela waved to Hilary across the High Street.

"Hilary, you don't know anyone in Cambridge, do you?"

"No, No, Angela, I'm sure I don't. Unless Marcus does."

Angela was not convinced by her friend's answer. She seemed very nervous, and Angela could have sworn that the colouring of her face had changed. Something was going on.

Hilary was completely unnerved by her friend's question. What did she know? Who told her? Has Paul told everyone their secret? Well, he never promised. She really thought that he wouldn't hurt her. Only one thing for it. I will have to tell Marcus the whole story. I should have done it ages ago. We're strong. We have been married for years. He wouldn't leave the children and me, over this. The past doesn't matter. It wasn't my fault. I was just so ashamed of my family. Marcus had perfect parents.

Hilary decided to put her plan into action.

"Hello Aunty Mary. When can you and Uncle Phil come here and stay for the week-end?"

"Hilary, love. Did I hear you right? Are you finally inviting us to your swanky house? Are you sure that you want us there?"

"I know that you are, probably mad and upset with me but, I just didn't want Marcus finding out, you know. Well, I'll own up. I think that he may get to know that I have a brother. There has been talk, in the village."

"So, that's it, Hilary. You now want to tell the truth and need us for moral support."

"It's not that Auntie. I really want you and Uncle Phil to be part of our lives. I want this all out in the open so you can be. Andrew has even said that he will stay. You must understand."

"I do, Hilary. Really, I do. I will let Phil know and he will be delighted to come. Any time you want us. You just sort it out with yourselves and Andrew. See you soon."

Hilary's last obstacle was to hope that Marcus wouldn't object to her guests staying the weekend. One guest that Marcus didn't know existed.

"Marcus, guess who's coming to stay next week-end. We don't have any last minute plans, do we?"

"No, nothing in the diary. Don't keep me in suspense. Who is staying with us?"

"Mary and Phil. You know my Auntie and Uncle."

"What, we haven't seen them since our wedding."

"No, complicated story. Andrew, my brother is staying as well."

"Your brother! You haven't got a brother. What's all this about, Hilary?"

"Have a drink, dinner will be a little while longer. I will tell you all about it. The girls are playing next door."

"My God, Hilary. What a story. It sounds like something out of a magazine. Why didn't you tell me all of this, before? When we met would have been a good time. Well, not exactly that night at the party. Sometime before we got engaged would have been good."

"Would you have still married me. That is what I was afraid of."

"Of course, I would have still married you. None of this was your fault. I bet you thought that my parents wouldn't approve if they knew, that's it. You couldn't have been more wrong. Why have you picked now to tell me?"

"I was hoping to keep the secret for life. It was a terrible coincidence that spoilt my plan. Paul Robertson was my brother's childhood friend. He spent a lot of time at our house until, well you know, the break up of my family. Paul said he wouldn't tell anyone but, Angela asked me the other day about Cambridge. I knew that someone had found out that I had been contacting Andrew. I assumed it must have been Paul. Then when I contacted Andrew, where he works in Cambridge, I noticed that my phone had been moved. It wasn't exactly where I had left it. I knew then that it was you who had asked Chris questions about Cambridge. I hadn't been in touch with Andrew, my own brother, since we both left home. I was lucky that his old college knew someone who knew where he worked, and they asked him to contact me. I panicked when Paul knew who I was and thought of Andrew. One other thing. If you are trying to put back something, exactly where you found it, remember what a tidy freak you are living with," Hilary laughed as Marcus kissed her hair."

"Well, I shall look forward to meeting your family," Marcus was relieved that his suspicions concerning his wife had solved a very old mystery, as well. Although, he still had the nagging doubts about his wife being involved in Paul's murder.

Chapter 5

James Watson grew up next door to Caroline Marshall. They went to the same schools and had always been friends. Their parents got on well and it was assumed that they would marry. A kind of arranged marriage, the bringing together of the families. Caroline's parents looked on James as a son and they were delighted that James was to become a policeman. What better match for their daughter than a pillar of the community. James joined the Specials as soon as he could.

Caroline loved James as the brother she had never had. She was sure she would marry James to keep everyone happy. She wasn't a confident life and soul of the party type of girl and being with James would mean she never had to attract a proper boyfriend. She wasn't in love with him but, did that matter?

"What time should I pick you up for the sixth form ball, tomorrow?" asked James.

"Oh, about 7pm will be fine. Dad said he will drop us off."

"See you then, bye," yelled James as he disappeared into the front hallway.

Caroline wore a simple, summer dress for the ball. She wasn't going to waste her money on a frivolous evening dress. Her friends would do that. They wanted to impress the boys they fancied. Caroline had no need to dress up for James and no one would fancy her, anyway. She wasn't unattractive. Just very shy.

"I'm not drinking. I'm working tomorrow so I need to keep a clear head," shouted James as they made their way to the noisy bar area.

"I don't really like alcohol. We only have a drink at Christmas. A coke is fine," replied Caroline, feeling ashamed of not drinking, like the rest of the group.

They found a quiet corner and sat hugging their cokes.

"You know that I am going to Nottingham University, don't you?" asked Caroline, knowing James would know because the whole street knew.

"Yes, I know but, you will be coming home a lot. Every weekend? Well, I'll be doing my police cadet training so, I might not be free every weekend. I'll let you know."

For the first time in her life, Caroline felt resentment towards James. How dare he tell her when to come home, just to see him. They were not even proper couple. They were eighteen years old and had never even kissed. She didn't want him to kiss her. She would come home when she wanted to see her parents and friends. Did James really care about her? He just cared about being a policeman. He probably wanted to be married so he could get a police house. He had life planned and she had no say in it.

Caroline's parents drove her to Nottingham and James was unable to go with them because her belongings took up the rest of the space in the car.

"I don't know how you are going to fit this lot into that tiny room," Caroline's mother had that hint of nagging in her voice as they registered.

"I will be fine, Mum, so will my stuff. Don't worry."

Caroline was worried. The least of her worries was where to fit her belongings. She was worried about the course, the socialising with other students, missing her Mum and Dad. She wasn't worried about stuff and she wasn't worried about missing James. The last box was unpacked. Her mother had folded every last piece of underwear, before placing it carefully in the drawer.

"You can go now. I'll be fine."

Caroline knew that if she didn't persuade her parents to leave, she would cry in front of them.

"If it's ok with you, Lovey, we will be on our way. Long journey back. Give your Mother a ring, soon." Her Father gave her a hug as he fetched the car keys out of his pocket.

"If you need anything or, are not happy we will be here. Just ring, anything." Her Mother was heading towards the door with tears rolling down her cheeks. "Oh Love, she's not the most confident of girls."

"She'll be fine. This will be the making of her. Don't fret. Leave her be."

Caroline wasn't fine for a couple of months but, she wanted her history degree, and she didn't want to worry her mother. She could cope with the course and the other students were friendly but, she didn't drink and stay up late. She would try and find a friend that didn't drink or party all night.

It was December and the first term was nearly over. Caroline was really looking forward to going home for Christmas. She had been home for a couple of weekends but, the train journey was long, and she felt she should try and cope, alone, at the week-ends. She did go shopping and for coffee with a couple of girls who had rooms near her. It was the evenings when she felt lonely and uncomfortable. Never mind, she thought. I can pack and study to avoid the Christmas parties. It was avoiding the Christmas parties that led to her life plans changing, forever.

"Oh, hello. I hope you don't mind me disturbing you but, I knew you were on your own. So am I and well, I thought we might have coffee in the kitchen," said the young man, nervously.

"Yes, no I don't mind you disturbing me. How did you know I was alone?" enquired Caroline, rather indignantly.

"Sorry, that makes me sound like a stalker. It's just that I heard the others trying to persuade you to go to the party, just after giving up on me."

"Oh, so there is another student on the planet that doesn't drink and party." Caroline was amused at her own reply.

"Afraid so. Sorry to disappoint you if you thought that you were unique."

"Well, coffee in the kitchen, then. I'm Caroline."

"I've got the coffee and the mugs. I'm Nick."

Caroline couldn't believe her luck. She had never been so relaxed in a boy's company. Apart from James but, that was different. She also noticed how good looking her new friend was. They chatted for ages and Nick pecked her on the cheek as he left her door and walked, to the door on the opposite side of the corridor, to his room. Just my luck, thought Caroline. Things are looking up and I'm going home. Nick will go home and forget who I am in January.

The train journey was as boring as ever. It was now cold, just to add to the discomfort. Caroline sat staring out of the window into the darkness of the bleak December evening. She couldn't stop thinking about Nick. He was good looking, charming and rather shy, like herself.

Christmas didn't seem the same, this year. The relatives came on Christmas day. James and his parents came Christmas morning for drinks, as usual. James was the same, arranging dates for them. It was Boxing Day when yet more relatives arrived. This was Dad's side of the family. The same procedure every year. Mum's relations Christmas Day and Dad's lot Boxing Day. Mum never minded the extra work and as Caroline was an only child she enjoyed the attention and presents. As they sat eating even more turkey for lunch Auntie Kay made a remark that made Caroline realise that she was going to have to disappoint everyone.

"I suppose when you come back from Uni. You and James will plan the wedding?"

No one was shocked by Auntie Kay's question. Only Caroline.

"Yes, we will start the ball rolling," chipped in Dad. "That lads doing really well at police college. He'll make our Caroline a good husband and a good son-in-law for us. Won't he love."

Caroline had never been a drama queen. She had never had a broken romance to cry over but, now she didn't know how to cope. She wouldn't leave the table. She wouldn't embarrass herself or, her family but, she knew that she couldn't marry James. She told the guests she needed a glass of water. She moved quickly into the kitchen. The glass slipped from her hands and she could feel the tears burning her face. Her mother, surprised and anxious, came in when she heard the glass shatter.

"Are you ok, love? You didn't look well in there."

"Yes, I'll be fine. I think I've got one of those viruses. A lot of colds and flu go around universities this time of year, you know."

"Of course they do, sweetheart. You have probably been working too hard, as well. Do you want a lie down? Nobody will mind. You just get better. You are going out with James tomorrow. You get yourself fit," said her mother as she patted her arm.

Caroline sat on her bed wishing she had Nick's telephone number. He would understand. Would he really? He hardly knows her. He will probably never speak to her again, apart from Hello. She was kidding herself. Nick could never feel the same way about her as she did him. This was still no reason to let everyone believe that she would marry James. She cried herself to sleep.

The next day Caroline went for a walk with James, and he told her about his career expectations. He never, once, asked about her course or her hopes for the future. He then suggested that their relationship should move onto a more intimate level. He said he had really missed her and realised he was in love with her. Caroline felt the panic she had experienced the day before. How could she let everyone down? What future did she have with Nick, anyway? She would pull herself together and go along with the plans. James already knew that his own and Caroline's parents were going out together on New Year's Eve. He saw this as his opportunity to have his first sexual encounter with Caroline. He knew she wouldn't be partying. This was his chance to make love to the woman that he was going to marry.

"Do you want to come round on New Year's Eve? I will cook for us and we will have the house to ourselves."

"Yes, ok," said Caroline reluctantly. "I haven't got any other plans. Yes, that would be lovely."

New Year's Eve arrived quicker than Caroline would have hoped. Her Mum was tarting herself up, as she called it.

"I hear James is cooking for you, tonight. It would be good for the two of you to have time to yourselves, if you know what I mean," giggled her mother.

"God, Mum, you are supposed to be the sensible one. It sounds as though you are encouraging me to go to bed with him."

"I was around in the sixties. Broad minded. Anyway, he will be the only one."

Caroline went to her room. She wouldn't bother to get changed. She would do what was what was expected of her. Lie back and think of England. She was just going to please everyone but herself. She slowly and reluctantly walked to her neighbour's front door.

"Hello, take a seat. Dinner is all under control."

Yes, all under control. Just like she was, thought Caroline.

"This is delicious. I didn't know you could cook. Did your Mum teach you?"

"You fill find out more about my many talents soon," replied James in a tone that unnerved Caroline.

Caroline ate slowly, trying to put off the moment. She offered to wash up. Make coffee. Should she feign illness? This virus won't go away. They sat on the settee, chatting like the old friends that they were. James touched her hair with his lips, moving slowly towards her mouth. To her surprise, his kiss wasn't what she had expected. She enjoyed his touch. She couldn't blame the alcohol. She hadn't touched a drop. As his hands moved over her body she began to relax. He led her by the hand to his bedroom. As he undressed her, she helped to speed up the process. As her hands reached for the zip of his trousers' she felt her whole body want him. As James lowered her onto the bed, she knew that this was what she wanted. James was now her lover. This was it. All thoughts of what, in her imagination, could have been with Nick, had gone.

Caroline and James spent the rest of the holiday together when he wasn't training. This was what she wanted. After University she would get a job, here, in her home town. Life would be perfect, and her family would be happy.

Caroline, reluctantly, caught the train to Nottingham. James had time to take her to the station and arranged to visit her a few weekends. As the train pulled out of the station, she waved to the man that she was going to marry.

The course was difficult and, luckily for Caroline, very time consuming. She still didn't feel the need to socialise but, was happier now she knew her destiny. She would finish her degree but, hoped it wouldn't be many years before she could become a full time Mum. She couldn't wait for James to visit.

It was early one evening when Caroline had settled down, lying on the bed, with her note pad, pens and books surrounding her, when there was a tap at the door.

"Oh, hello. I haven't seen you since the beginning of term."

"No, I didn't come back for a couple of weeks. I had a bad dose of flu. It started on New Year's Day. I was going to contact you over Christmas but, being the idiot that I am, forgot to get your number."

Caroline invited Nick into her room. She was surprised to see him and, even more surprised that she still found him very attractive. She wanted to be with him despite her relationship with James changing. She offered Nick coffee and chocolate biscuits. They chatted, just like the first time. In fact, the only time they had met. She was disappointed when he left and, her confused state of mind resulted in a sleepless night. Did she want to sleep with Nick? Could she be in love with two men? What did she mean? She didn't even know Nick. Anyway, he was just a friend. Someone, like herself, who wanted a quieter life whilst studying. He just happened to be a very attractive friend of the opposite sex. She wouldn't tell James about Nick. Even though there was nothing to tell. James is possessive, anyway. She doesn't want complications. She will tell Nick about James. Nick is a friend. He won't care is she has a boyfriend. He may be gay. It is all in her imagination. Nick probably doesn't fancy her, anyway.

James arrived on a Friday evening in January. As Caroline led him along the corridor to her room Nick came out of his room.

"Hello, this must be James. I've heard all about you, mate." Nick greeted him cheerily.

"Who's that? He knows all about me."

"Oh, that's Nick. His room is just across the hall from mine. He's just another student. You know, we all share the kitchen and that. Of course, I told him about you. You're my boyfriend." Caroline was nervous and not prepared for meeting Nick on James's arrival.

"Do you see a lot of him, then?"

She could tell that James was jealous already. It wouldn't be the last of his questions.

"No, I told you, we see everyone in the kitchen. Well, yes, actually, I do see him a lot. He opens his door when I open mine," she said, sarcastically. "Its's how it is, being a student."

The first weekend together didn't go as she had hoped. The jealous doubts in his mind would not go away. They made love, just like the first time but, she knew James was tense.

"Do you really need this degree? I'll get a good salary. Promotions can be regular in the police force. If you work hard and know what you are doing you can be on a good salary in no time. That will be me."

Caroline was shocked by his question.

"What brought this on? Of course, I am finishing my degree. In this day and age women are educated. In case you didn't know. They are not tied to the kitchen sink. I don't care what salary you earn. I may want a job where I earn even more than you. You just wait and see."

James left early on the Sunday. Caroline's doubts had returned. How dare he treat her like a kept woman. We weren't even married, yet. She was taking a step backwards. Before they had become lovers, she knew he was controlling. Had she been taken in by sex. Sex and friendship was all they had. It may sound a good basis for marriage but, she felt she couldn't trust him. I can have sex with anyone, she thought. This was unlike Caroline to even think of such things but, she wanted her degree. She wanted Nick. Did she? He wouldn't control her. How did she know? She was young. She could be a career woman. Why bother with either of them?

James did visit a few weekends but, they mostly stayed in her room. She knew this was to keep her away from Nick. The sex was still great but, she was back to her original feelings regarding her relationship with James. They would never marry.

Caroline and Nick saw a lot of each other, and she felt more comfortable with him than anyone else in her life. One evening Nick told her he was falling in love with her.

"I don't know what to do," said Caroline, tearfully.

"You don't have to do anything but, if you don't feel the same and I can't compete with James, just say so."

"I'm very fond of you, Nick. I have to marry James. Our families are expecting it." Caroline was almost hysterical. This is what she had wanted for months. She wanted Nick to love her but, why did he have to tell her he loved her, now. She was confused. She didn't want either of them.

"Well, to be honest I was prepared for this. I've told you now so, that's it. Perhaps it's better if we don't see each other. Goodbye, Caroline. Best of luck."

Caroline stood in front of the door.

"What do you mean? It's best if we don't see each other. We can't avoid each other. How can you be so stupid?" Tears ran down her cheeks as she shouted at Nick. She allowed Nick to leave the room and threw herself on the bed, sobbing uncontrollably.

What am I doing? This isn't me. Mousy little Caroline was never going to be fought over by two men. A few months ago, I would never have been in this situation. She wasn't going to spend time with Nick ever again. It was a few weeks until James's next visit. Was that it?

Did she just want whoever was available? Really? Was that really what she wanted?

Caroline could always concentrate on her work. In her brief lapses of concentration, she thought of Nick. Should she knock on his door? Would he believe her that she wanted him and not James? She could send a letter to James. The trouble at home would have time to die down before she got home for the Easter break. The coward's way out, she knew but, what else could she do?

"Oh, it's you. Everything ok?"

"I want to speak to you, Nick Can I come in?"

"Yes, coffee?"

A few weeks ago, you told me that you loved me. Is that still true? I have written to James to tell him it's finished between us." The words tumbled out of Caroline's mouth.

"Phew, ah. This is a lot to take in. I'll just get the coffee. I'm not used to all of this drama," said Nick as the boiling water flowed over the rim of the cup.

"I'm sorry. I just can't help laughing. It's just nerves, really. I hope you didn't scold yourself with the water. You won't believe me but, I'm really not a drama queen, either, really."

Nick put his arms around Caroline and held her tightly. He knew that most men would have told her where to go. He wasn't that sort. He was too shy to have the ladies fighting him off. No, this was the one. He wasn't going to ruin his chances and let pride get in his way. They kissed each other passionately and Caroline spent the night in his cramped bed. I can't believe this. What a slut I am. Caroline woke up during the night troubled by her conscience. I have never slept with anyone until New Year's Eve. It's not even Easter and I have slept with two.

James never contacted her, and she hoped that he didn't really care about her. His police career would mean the world to him. Perhaps he had realised that Nick was more than just, someone in the kitchen. James may not have contacted her but, trouble was waiting for her when she arrived home for the holiday. She had had letters from her mother asking her what she was playing at.

"What do you mean, you've met someone else? Who, when do we meet him?"

"I'm not sure when Mum. It's a bit awkward with James living next door."

"Have you slept with him?"

"Yes Mum. You know, you lived through the sixties, remember."

"How dare you behave like that?"

"It's not like that. We really love each other. James and I were only friends. We were forced into a relationship. You know that. You and your meddling sisters. James and his interfering parents. You all forced me. I only went along with it because I didn't want to upset anyone. I thought I'd never find anyone to really love me. Now I have and I would be really happy Mum but, I need your blessing and, Dad's."

"We'll see. I just hope you know what you're doing. Me and your Dad have to live with this, you know."

Caroline and Nick married a few years after they had finished University. Caroline got a brilliant job, in her words, in a museum. Perfect use of her degree. Nick was happy for her to work. Caroline's parents excepted him for the nice young man that he was. They remained friends with James and his parents. James seemed to get over Caroline very quickly. He didn't want a serious relationship as his career was his life. He didn't progress as fast as he had led Caroline to imagine but, he had been promoted. The drama that Caroline had envisaged between both families had never materialised which made her realise that, perhaps, James was just trying to please his family, as well, and never really loved her. All's well that ends well was the saying that sprang to her mind. Caroline and Nick bought a house on the new development at Barker's End, a few miles from Newston. Nick worked hard and, together with their two daughters, had a happy family life.

Caroline had taken her girls to visit her parents. Sophie and Millie loved playing with their Grandad so, Caroline took the opportunity of free time to go shopping. James had finished his police training in the nearby town. His job had lived up to his expectations. The local residents remembered him as a child and he gained a lot of respect as the local police officer. This and his enthusiasm helped him to gain promotion.

"Hello, I haven't seen you for ages. How's things?"

"Oh, hello James. I expected to see you in uniform. You are still a policeman? Mum never said you had left the force."

"Oh yes, I wouldn't leave the job for the world. Detective Sergeant now. Out of Uniform. You and, what's his name? ok. Nick, that's it, Nick. You two alright?"

"Yes, everything is ok with us. Just visiting Mum and Dad. The girls are with them now. You could pop in and see us. I am sure you know where we live. Mum tells me you have a nice, swanky flat in town."

"Yes, and I would love to see where you live. I'll take you up on that offer and call in for coffee one day."

Oh, what have I done, thought Caroline as she made her way back to the car park? Why did I suggest he visit? Do I really want him back in my life? Will he just be my friend again?

A few months after her encounter with James Caroline was gardening when an unfamiliar car pulled up near her driveway. Oh no, it really is him. If only I had been in the back garden, I could have pretended I wasn't in. Stupid, stupid idea to invite him here.

"Oh, hello. I didn't expect you to come." Of course you did, Caroline, she mumbled to herself.

"I have a free day so couldn't refuse an offer from such a dear friend."

Caroline knew by the tone of his voice that this wouldn't go well. What she couldn't foresee was her own reaction to the situation.

"Lovely house. You've done well for yourself."

"Yes, well we have worked hard. Nick works very hard. Coffee? Please sit down."

It must have been the bored housewife syndrome. What else could have made her do it? She remembered every details of their brief sex life. When she sat near him, drinking coffee and chatting, she knew it wouldn't take much persuasion on his part, to sleep with him. She was perfectly happy with Nick. Of course she was. He was the love of her life but, he worked away from home, more than she would have liked. The girls, on her own, were a handful. Don't make excuses, Caroline. As they made their way to the bedroom. Her bedroom, she shared with Nick, her excitement trembled through her body. Sex with James was just how it used to be. She was eighteen, again.

"Well, that was a pleasant surprise. I can't wait for my next day off."

"No, please don't come here again. It was a terrible mistake. Please just forget everything that happened."

"It didn't seem like a mistake in that bedroom. I didn't exactly rape you, Caroline. Bye, see you again. As soon as I can."

I can't believe what I have just done but, Caroline knew that she would do it again, and again. Caroline, in a state of panic, phoned her friend.

"Hi, Angela. Could you do me a favour and pick the girls up from school for me? That's if you're not busy. A cup of tea in it for you. Maybe a glass of wine."

"You know I'll collect those little Angels, anytime but, you're not usually an afternoon wine drinker. Everything ok."

"Yes, fine. See you later."

"You two go and play in the garden. It's a lovely afternoon."

"Mum, can we take a drink out? We won't break the glass."

"Caroline, what's wrong? Why couldn't you get the girls?"

"I thought you didn't mind, fetching them, I mean. I had a visitor."

"Oh, anyone I know?"

"Oh, Angela. I've got to tell you. Let me just top up the glasses. I don't know where to start."

"Come on Caroline. You can tell me anything I won't tell a soul."

Caroline knew her best friend knew all the village gossip. She was popular and lively. She knew she could trust her but, this was so out of character for Caroline that Angela would never believe her.

"You remember I told you about my old boyfriend. You know my childhood sweetheart. If you could call him that."

Angela knew that she wasn't going to hear good news. She had easily guessed why her friend was so troubled.

"Yes. I remember. Watch it! Are we going to drink the whole bottle before 4 O'clock?"

"Oh, Angela. He came here this afternoon and we went to bed." There, that's it. I've said it, sobbed Caroline as she finished the contents of her glass.

"What you? Sweet, innocent little Caroline. You must have had a sleep this afternoon and this was a dream." Angela made her reply sound convincing but, she knew this was the news her friend was so anxious to tell her.

"I wish it was."

"Well, not much shocks me, but."

"You can't be as shocked as I am. The point is, it gets worse."

"Worse? How much worse. You're not running away together, are you?"

"Don't be silly. No it's just that I really enjoyed it and given the chance, I'd do it again, I think."

"Caroline!, Anyone but you. Well just be careful and if it's what you really want, it's up to you."

"I would never hurt Nick and, no, it's not what I really want but, it seems like a drug. I could never resist. Anyway, I might never see him again."

Caroline and James met regularly for sex. Her friend, Angela was the only person who knew of her affair and that's how Caroline was going to keep it.

James had never shown his resentment of the fact that he had lost the love of his life. He had dated a few girls but, was never seriously involved with any of them. He loved his job. He had a good social life with his colleagues and he wasn't prepared to work at a relationship with a woman. Caroline had always been there when they were growing up. She was, literally, the girl next door. They were real friends, and he couldn't believe his luck that New Year's Eve when they became lovers. Nick came along and spoilt everything. He would never let his family know but, he wasn't going to be treated like that. He would bide his time and win her back. It was his lucky day when he bumped into her in town. She still felt the same way about him. This was a nice little arrangement for Caroline but, he would make her see sense and one day she would leave Nick for him. He'd take care of the girls. He really did love Caroline.

James good fortune, or so he saw it, was to come in the guise of Paul's murder.

Two men in Barker's End both shared the same problem. Marcus and Nick were both happily married, family men. Or, at least they were. They both had lovely wives that they adored. Women they could trust. Or could they?

Marcus and Nick had only ever been drinking and cricket mates. Like a lot of men on the new estate, they didn't have close friends. They never discussed each other's thoughts or fears. Who was going to win the Premiership? Would it be Manchester City or Liverpool? Did Chelsea have a chance? Poor old Manchester United didn't stand a chance, again. They would be great again, one day. Their time will come. The men would laugh as they enjoyed a pint. Did you know you could now get that on an App? The help and advice that they would give each other. The competition between them. Who was more up to date with the latest technology? Dave had just had his company car upgraded. Did you see him come home the other evening? The two men had chatted at Angela's and Chris's dinner parties but, Angela and Chris invited everyone.

Nick was aware that his wife, Caroline didn't like Marcus's wife, Hilary. Caroline thought that Hilary was far too snooty. She was sure that she looked down on her. The men stayed out of these female squabbles. They were simply happy with work, family, a few pints and a bit of banter.

Marcus and Nick didn't know that they both suspected that their wives were involved in Paul Robertson's death. Of course, neither of them actually thought that they were capable of murder but, their strange behaviour seemed connected.

Hilary was so adamant that she wanted the extension built but, when Marcus told her to go ahead and hire Robertson, she was very reluctant.

Nick's suspicious started before the murder. Why was Caroline spending so much money? Or, at least, withdrawing so much. There was no evidence that she was spending it.

Why is she taking that money out of her savings account? What is she buying? This is unlike her. Nick is wracking his brain, as he works out the finances.

I can't ask her, said Nick to himself as he looked again at the savings account statement. We have always trusted each other. It will all "come out in the wash," I'm sure. I can't ask Angela. Angela knows everything about Caroline. She might, inadvertently, mention that I was asking questions.

Nick knows everything about Caroline. She is an open book or, at least she was until a few months before Paul Robertson was murdered. Of course, she is not a murderer but, neither is Nick and, that didn't stop them questioning him. All these thoughts are going through Nick's mind as he studies the bank statements. It is the same amount every month and then the withdrawals stop. I won't ask her. I trust her and, for all I know she may be saving for a big family holiday. A party for my birthday. A big surprise. She has moved the money. Opened another account so I don't know what she is doing. I don't want to spoil it all. No, I won't ask her. Caroline is so careful with money. She has been saving this since we were first married. Not even the cost of bringing up two daughters has dented her efforts. Perhaps that's it. This would be University fees saved for the girls. This is typical of Caroline. She is so efficient and prepared. The money will not be spent on anything reckless. Caroline hasn't got a reckless bone in her body. Nick got on with balancing the finances and forgot the whole thing.

There was something else that was bothering Nick. He knew that James Watson was coming to the house when he was working away. How did he know? This was a village. He overheard the Mum's natter when he took the girls to school, one morning. He knew that they were talking about James visiting Caroline. For a start, they all stopped talking and changed the subject when he walked past. He heard, too, that she was mousey and couldn't possibly having an affair. He knew what they thought of Caroline. She wasn't like them and, he was glad. She had known James since they were children. Nick knew that. Yes, there was talk of them getting married. It would have just been a marriage of convenience. This was expected by the two families. After he came along all that changed. He and Caroline fell in love. Their life was happy. Why didn't she tell him that James was visiting? He knew that they were friends.

Nick Freeman's misgivings would not be solved, easily.

Chapter 6

John and Jenny met when they were both at nursery school. Met, wasn't exactly the right word. Their mothers walked the school route together. They couldn't avoid each other. At four years old sexual attraction didn't come into it. They were play mates. The village was so small that anybody to play with was a bonus. As they settled into primary school, John and Jenny preferred to spend school break time mixing with their own sex. In fact, John thought that all girls were silly cry babies. Jenny announced to her Mum that boys, including John, were boring and dirty. At least, this is what she led the popular girls at school to believe. Secretly, she still enjoyed John's company. John was fun. He made things out of wood. She felt enormously proud when she, a silly girl, was allowed into the shed. He even let her hold his models together, after he had applied the glue. John could never admit this to his friends but, he didn't think that Jenny was silly. He had never seen her cry. Jenny loved playing football. Other girls had dolls and jewellery making kits. Jenny had toy cars, lorries and a tool set. At the weekends and after school John and Jenny couldn't be separated.

John and Jenny started to go to school dances together when they were at secondary school. The cinema in Newston was another popular night out.

John could afford to treat Jenny. He was an apprentice carpenter at a local building firm. They never went out on dates with other people. They were the best of friends and they fell in love.

This popular young couple, who lived in Barker's End got engaged before they were twenty years old. This was the beginning of a love story that was to last.

"Jenny, I can't help it. Don't you think that I'd work if I could?" John Gilbert put down his knife and fork as he pleaded with his wife for sympathy.

"I know, John, it's just that I do as much as I can. I'm cleaning ten houses, including the doctor's surgery. With the kids to look after and this place to keep clean, I'm doing my best."

"I know, I know. Don't you think I feel bad enough letting my wife keep me. I might have to try further-a-field. See if I can get work on housing developments. I will do some research. If necessary, just go where the work is. I might have to stay away from home during the week but, it will be worth it. I'll find something, Jen, don't worry."

John and Jenny Gilbert had been married for fifteen years. They had both lived in Barker's end all their lives. Their families had lived on the same housing estate as where John and Jenny now lived with their family. Jenny had worked as an accounts clerk before she had her first child. She had never wanted to return to work but, needed to and was lucky enough to find cleaning jobs in the village. She wanted to be close to her children. Three of them were now at the local primary school, with the eldest boy now at Secondary School. She was really happy. John and her children were her life, and she would do all she could to help with the family income.

John Gilbert was a carpenter. He served an apprenticeship when he left school. He loved working with wood. He, with Jenny's support, became self-employed ten years ago. He was fortunate that a new housing estate was going to be built at Barker's End. The work was on his doorstep. The building company wanted contractors for everything: Electricians, plumbers, carpenters, bricklayers. Everything was looking up for the Gilberts. They had got two children by then. John could work as much overtime as he wanted too. He could still be home in time to read his toddlers a story before bedtime. Jenny had started cleaning for the "posh" ladies who had already moved into the new houses. Life couldn't be better. Jenny was pregnant with her third child but, her parents were always willing to help with childcare. They loved being grandparents. Looking after the children was not a chore. John's parents were older but, the love for their grandchildren wasn't any less. The practical chores were just left to the other grandparents. This is what they both wanted. John and Jenny had both agreed on having four children.

John was a hardworking, popular man. After the new houses had been completed, he found plenty of local work. His customers liked that fact that he had grown up in the village. A local lad. John and Jenny were now the proud parents of four children, two boys and two girls. A newcomer to the area was about to cause problems, unexpectedly, to their lifestyle.

"Hello, Mrs Armstrong. When do you want me to fit that kitchen? I can get the cupboards and store them in your garage, if that's ok with you? When you give me the go ahead, I'll hire a skip and rip out the old one.

I bet you're excited. You girls love a new kitchen, I know," John chatted excitedly to his latest customer.

"Would you like a cup of tea, John?"

"Yes, lovely. You know how many sugars," John laughed.

"Yes, sit down, dear."

"Everything all right, Mrs Armstrong? No problem with the dates, is there?"

"Look John. I don't know how to say this but, I've had a better quote for the kitchen. You know I want you to do it. I've been friends with Jenny's Mum for years. It's just that he's a lot cheaper, this chap. People say that he is good."

"Oh, I didn't know that I had competition," John tried to sound light hearted.

John went home and told Jenny the news. He had to tell her. She knew that something was wrong.

"I didn't know that there was anyone else local, who was a carpenter. Did you know anyone when you were working on the estate?"

"There were lots of blokes. They came and went. I can't remember all of them. Just had a laugh with them. You know how it is."

"Well, I'll get to hear from the "posh" ladies. I'll do some digging. He probably won't be around for long. Jenny, as usual, had an answer. John carried on doing quotes for work for people who had known him since he was a child.

"Hello, John. Do come in. Have a cup of tea."

"Hi, Fred. Is it all the window frames you want me to replace? I'm glad you don't want this plastic rubbish. Nice wooden frames. Keep the character of the place. I'm glad that we have to."

"John, I had another quote. This chap can do other little jobs for me. A bit of plumbing. Fix the electrics. Sorry, John. It's just me pension doesn't go that far. I've got to be careful. A lad like you will get plenty of work. No hard feelings, aye son?"

"Of course, you have to be careful. Fred. Just one thing. What's the chap's name?"

"Paul, something or other. Quiet bloke."

"Thanks for the tea, Fred. Let me know if you need anything else doing."

"Bye lad and sorry."

John, yet again had to break the bad news to Jenny.

"That's two customers lost. I just know his name is Paul. There was a Paul working on the development. He never really joined in with us other lads."

"Was he a carpenter?" asked Jenny.

"No, well guess he did everything. Plumbing, bricklaying, the lot, I think."

"That's it, then. Jack of all trades. Master of none. People will soon get fed up with him."

"Jen, they say he's good. Did you get any information from the women you clean for?"

"I do know that some of them are having someone build conservatories and extensions. You know that sort of thing. They have got notes by the telephone to ring, but no name. Just says call builder."

"We will just have to make more enquiries. I can't afford to lose much more work. Someone must know him."

John had to face many more rejections. Of course, I understand, he would say to people who had known him all of his life. You have every right to get as many quotes as you like, was his answer to his old friends.

He wasn't going to alienate them. This Paul wouldn't stick around. One evening John made an announcement, which surprised his wife.

"Jenny, I'm going up the pub after dinner."

"John, you never go up the pub. We can't afford for you to go up the pub."

"This is in the name of research. He's bound to go in the pub."

"Who is?"

"This fantastic mystery builder."

"Well, if you say so. Don't be late and don't drink too much," Jenny shouted as her husband made his way into the village.

John was right. He recognised him sitting at a table, all alone, with a pint in his hand.

"Hi mate. I thought I recognised you. Paul isn't it? We worked on the new houses together." John was friendly and chatty to his rival.

"If you say so. I haven't got your memory. Didn't have much to do with the other blokes."

"No, I remember that. You could do all the job's, though?"

"Yeah, pretty much. Are you offering work, then?"

No, I just heard that you're getting a lot of work round here."

Yeah well. What's it got to do with you? I'm getting off to me bed, now. A busy day ahead." Paul finished his drink and put the glass down heavily on the table."

If he wasn't such a miserable ba…, thought John, I would ask if I could work with him but, I couldn't stick that all day. John left the pub, soon after Paul. He could only afford half a pint and his research project had paid off. He knew who his rival was.

"Hi Jen, I did find out who the mystery builder is. He's the one off the site who I thought it was. I don't know his surname, though. He's not very talkative, to say the least."

"Well, I told you, he'll probably move on. He's not local like you. You'll get your customers back. Just be patient. I'm off to bed."

John wasn't as confident as Jenny. He'd heard talk from the locals. It seems the stranger could do no wrong. John decided he would just have to undercut his quotes. He would concentrate on the carpentry jobs, only. Yet another plan didn't work.

"Sorry John but, Paul can do the lot, so it keeps the costs down."

"Yes, I realise, I thought that it was Paul, said John, knowing full well it was always the same person that was doing all of the work. John was confident his next plan would work and was eager to tell Jenny.

"I'll try in the town, tomorrow. The bigger building firms may be offering work."

"Good idea, love."

John did get some work in the local town. The largest building firm in the area was restoring an old block of local authority houses. If John could supply good references, he could have a trial period and work on the new kitchens.

"I told you it would all work out," said Jenny, cheerfully, as she peeled the potatoes.

"Yes, you were right. Not sure how long it will last. I'll just have to wait and see. They may like what I do and offer me more work."

Jenny had popped into the High Street shop for milk. Dave's shop sold everything. A loaf of bread or, a packet of nails. If you needed it, Dave could get it for you. Unlike a lot of village stores, Dave's was always busy. The locals new that they had to use it or lose it.

"Hello Jenny. Julie wants a word. Go into the back room. I'll let her know that you are here."

Jenny and Julie, Dave's wife, had been friends for years. They didn't spend a lot of time together. Jenny was too busy with work and the children. Julie worked in the shop seven days a week.

"Jen, I know that you ae a good cleaner. You don't want another job, do you?"

"Julie, I've already got ten cleaning jobs. Five days a week, morning and afternoon. Why?"

"Dave and I are doing well in the shop but, I never get time to clean the flat or, even sit down. I just thought, I don't mind cleaning but, I don't have the time."

"Julie, I've had an idea. Of course, you will have to ask Dave and you both have to agree."

"Well, what's your grand plan?"

"If you actually like cleaning, I could work in the shop, say 2/3 evenings, so you could have time in the flat. I know I am a good cleaner but, a change working in the shop would be good for me and John, or my Mum, can mind the kids in the evening. What do you think?"

"I don't mind but let's see if Dave has a free moment for a chat. You don't want to talk to John, first?"

"No, John will be fine. John hasn't got much work, at the moment. We need every penny we can get. I did cashiering before I had the kids. I'd be good with the till."

"I'm sure that you would be." Dave and Julie agreed that their friend would be trustworthy and friendly to the customers.

"We can only pay you the going rate for cleaning, though. That's what we budgeted for."

John, reluctantly, agreed with the plans. He knew that Julie was already working too hard but, they needed the money. The job would give her a break from the house. A change from cleaning, for her, and people to talk too.

"Jenny, the job on the old houses finishes next week. I will have to try and work away. I don't have a choice."

"If you work away who will look after the kids in the evening, when I am working?"

"Your Mum would love to do it. You know that she loves them to bits. I know that you don't like relying on her but, we don't have a choice. She'll understand."

"Yes, you're right. We don't have any options, do we? I was afraid that this was coming. We'll cope. We always do. That Paul chap will be gone soon. Just you wait and see."

John searched the vacancies, for carpenters, the length and breadth of the country. He finally got an interview for a job that was about one hundred miles from home. He got the job, and it was at least six months work. The money was more than he had ever made in his life. Jenny wasn't pleased but, she knew she had no choice. John came home early Friday evenings and left every Sunday, after lunch. Jenny missed her husband, even though he phoned her every evening. Her Mum was a great help, practically and emotionally. John's bed and breakfast accommodation was clean and the food was good. The landlady always cooked him an evening meal. He worked long days so, during the week he just worked, ate and slept. This suited him. The other lads, on the site, were friendly and were always inviting him for a drink but, money for his family was his only objective.

Jenny was enjoying her work in the village store. She used any spare moment to tidy the shelves or, she would ask Dave's permission to implement any changes that she thought may bring in more customers. Julie loved her new found freedom, in the evenings that Jenny worked. One evening, when Jenny was alone in the store, he came in to buy a chocolate bar. She didn't know who he was, at first. He wasn't a local, that is residents of the village who were born and bred there, like herself. Jenny didn't think that he came from the new estate. He was too rough.

"Dave, I didn't recognise him. Do you know who he was?"

Dave had come out from the back room as the mystery customer took his change.

"Yes, he doesn't have much to say for himself but, Julie told me his name. He comes in quite a lot, in the evenings. It's Paul. The one who's doing the building work for those rich, bored, housewives."

"Oh, that's him is it?"

After that evening Jenny served Paul regularly. He bought snacks and fizzy drinks. Paul hardly spoke. Please, thank you and exchanging coins. Jenny couldn't help disliking Paul. He was responsible for her family's misfortune. He was the reason her husband wasn't at home. Even if she didn't blame him for everything, he was still an unpleasant man. Dave had noticed Jenny's hostile attitude towards Paul. Dave was fond of Jenny. She was efficient, friendly and the till always balanced. She was also someone who is wife could moan too.

"Jen, love. These things happen in business. It's not Paul's fault that he is good at his job."

"Are you saying that my John isn't a good worker?"

"No, of course he's a good worker. If another shop opened in the village, I'd have to cope, improve and do whatever it takes."

Jenny started to cry and then apologised to Dave for her unprofessional behaviour.

"I don't think he will stick around here. John will be ok. Trust your old Uncle Dave."

Jenny felt better and she knew she would have to be strong when John came home at the weekend. Perhaps she could persuade her husband to change tactics. Diversify.

"John, there is something we should discuss, after dinner."

"Oh no, you've been thinking. That's trouble."

"Right then. Dinner won't be long and then we can have that chat."

"I've been driving for over four hours. Traffic is murder on a Friday. Let me have a cup of tea first. Can I at least take my coat off?"

After dinner Jenny broached the subject.

"You see, John. I've been thinking about Paul the builder. He can do anything but, you're the woodwork man. You could make nice furniture for the people in the posh houses. Build wardrobes, fitted kitchens. Something different. Even garden furniture. Real rich people don't want what you can get in the shops."

"Hang on, Jen. I'd need special tools and equipment for that sort of stuff. I'll need a bigger workshop than the garage. Not to mention the money to set all this up. Where can we get that from?"

"I've thought of that as well. Mum and Dad will help, and they would have a purpose built workshop for you, on the land by the side of their house."

"Jen, you've got this all worked out but, how do you know I will get the customers. It's not that simple."

John liked his wife's idea but, you must have the market for this kind of furniture. He didn't want to be in debt with his in-laws. He didn't mind asking them to do the odd bit of baby-sitting but, this was different. He may have the expertise but, he didn't have the confidence to start this up. He had no idea about marketing. Jen would be good at this sort of thing but, she was far too busy. No, he would stick to working away from home. The money was good and he had got used to the travelling. He didn't need any more complications in his life.

The time that John had dreaded had come. The work on the site was finished. John would have to find work in another part of the country. Jenny understood his reluctance to start again, making bespoke furniture. She had got carried away with her big ideas. John just wasn't the type. He wasn't a brash, confident salesman. She just had to hope and keep telling herself and John that everything would work out. Even Dave agreed with them that Paul would move on. John's work finally finished. He was unable to find other work. Jenny must remain strong. She still had her jobs. They only bought essentials. The children didn't care, Well, Jack the eldest, was a typical teenager. He was always asking for money. He knew the financial situation and his paper round money bought most of what he wanted. The children seemed to sense that their family love would keep everything going. Both Jenny and John's parents had offered money. John wouldn't take it but, he may have to for the sake of his children.

Jenny's contact with Paul was now more than selling him chocolate bars. The women on the new estate, who employed Paul to build, were the same women that Jenny cleaned for. Jenny's good fortune was, that after Paul had finished his work, Jenny was needed to carry out one-off cleaning tasks, as well as her weekly cleaning. This could be week-end work and she was paid a lot extra. On more than one occasion she came into contact with Paul. She couldn't help it, she hated him. She didn't care if Dave said it was business. She hated the problems that he had caused her and her family. He was a nasty man, as well, she thought. He didn't speak. He was rude and moody. How could they employ him when her John was lovely! I wish he was dead, she thought, as she saw him leave a house, she was about to enter. She had asked her employer's why they had hired Paul. They all said he could do everything well. The friendlier women did giggle as they told her it was because they fancied him. How could they? He was their bit of rough. The moodiness added to the mystery. Well, they had time for that sort of thing. John was too friendly, too open and he wouldn't look at another woman. What if she tampered with Paul's work. Don't be silly, Jenny, someone may get hurt. A child, maybe, would be injured. Anyway, how would she know how to tamper with anything. She didn't let John know but, she was at her wits end.

When Jenny went to the shop, that evening, Julie came rushing out to meet her.

"Jenny, have you heard the news?"

"What news? I haven't heard anything. I've been at home all day. You know that my two youngest have been off school, today, with a cold. I've had to cancel all of my cleaning jobs." Jenny was intrigued by what Julie had to tell her.

"Paul, the builder Paul, who you don't like. He's been found dead in the woods."

"Julie, what do you mean? Found dead! Was he drunk? Did he get lost on the way home and die of hyperthermia or, alcohol poisoning?"

"Well, the rumours say he was murdered. That's not all, Jen. Some gossips in the shop have suggested, to the police, that your John may have something to do with his death. You know, because of him taking his work."

Julie! How could you?"

"Jen. It wasn't me or, Dave. We would never tell the police anything like that. When something like this happens the first place to come for information, true or false, is the village shop."

"Of course, Julie. I'm sorry. I suppose we will be getting a visit from the police, soon. We know that we are innocent so, I'm not worried. See you soon, Julie, bye."

Jenny was worried. She hated Paul. She blamed him for the struggle that her life had now became but, she would never hurt anyone. What about John, though, she thought to herself. She was worried sick about money and hardly slept at night. John was taking the situation much worse as he thought he had let his family down. How did she know how he was really feeling? Could he resort to drastic measures? She was glad that Paul was dead. This would solve their problems but, would it? She must stop thinking that her John was capable of murder.

"John, you've heard about Paul?"

John could hardly take his key out of the door when Jenny confronted him.

"Yes, I have. They say he was murdered. I can't say that I'm sorry."

"I feel the same but, the police may want to question us. You know, because of you losing work to Paul," Jenny spoke tentatively, trying to gauge her husband's reaction.

"We have nothing to hide. Let us just wait and see," John headed to the living room to greet his children. It wasn't long before Jenny's fears were realised.

"Mr. Gilbert? May we come in?"

"Yes, I know what you are here for. Take a seat."

"It has been brought to our attention that you may have a motive for killing Paul Robertson. Is that correct, Sir?"

"Yes, that is correct. Since he arrived here, he has been under cutting my quotes. The posh women on the estate hire him to do all the jobs around the house. If you ask me, I think that they fancy him. Bored housewives wanting a bit of excitement. I'm a carpenter. A good one but, I can't do the plumbing, electrics or the sex."

Jenny was surprised by her husband's directness to the police inspector. Discussing the women on the estate was, normally, something they laughed about in private.

"Yes, Mr. Gilbert, we can't speculate about the reasons that Mr Robertson was employed but, it is true that without him your life and finances would improve."

"Yes, I'm not sorry that he's dead but, I'm not a murderer. Things would have picked up. He would have moved on. He's not from around here."

"That's just it, Mr. Gilbert. We don't know much about him. Can you tell us where you were on the night of the 20th June? We don't know that Mr. Robertson was in the local pub that evening. The Landlord wasn't working and the bar staff don't know Paul. His body was found at 11am the next morning."

"I was here, with Jenny and the kids. Only Jenny can witness this. We were all in bed. Not much more that I can say."

"I presume, Mrs Gilbert, that you can verify this?"

"Yes, we go to bed about 10pm. John was working away a lot but, after he finished, he gets up early to look for work. He wasn't out. He doesn't go to the pub. We can't afford it."

"That's all for now. Thank you."

"I'm not sure about him boss. He seemed resentful of Paul, quite bitter. Perhaps it wasn't just the work. He might have wanted the posh women to fancy him," laughed James, the young detective.

"He did seem bitter but, he has lost a lot of work. You can see his point. This Paul, the builder doesn't seem very popular around here. I don't think that Gilbert murdered him but, we will do some more digging. Mrs Gilbert may have something to do with it."

DCI Stock decided to pay a visit to Mrs Gilbert, when she was alone.

"Hello, Mrs Gilbert. May we come in?"

"Yes but, John isn't in."

"It's you we have come to see."

"Me?"

"Yes. A local resident has told us that you were seen out, in the village, on the night of the murder. You were walking along the High Street around about midnight. Is that right, Mrs Gilbert?"

"I'm not going to lie to you. I just didn't want John to know. I haven't slept for weeks since John lost his work. I normally just lie there and worry or, get up and make a cup of tea. John carries on as normal, snoring away. It's funny that. Whatever worries you men, you still have the ability to sleep. If only I could do that. Anyway, that night, I was really agitated. It was warm and I had to get out. I've lived here all of my life. I'm never sacred of walking round the village, day or night. I know who saw me. It was old Jim. He was walking Benjy, his little dog. He didn't speak but, I knew he had spotted me. He is always out late. He says it suits him and Benjy. Too hot, when it's earlier. I swear I didn't murder Paul. I didn't even see him that night."

"If you can come down to the station with us for tests. Have you got the clothes and shoes you were wearing that evening, Mrs Gilbert?"

"Yes, I will do anything but, I must get my Mum to collect the kids from school and, I don't want John to know about this."

"Of course, phone your Mum. If you are innocent, Mrs Gilbert, nobody has to know anything. You may want to tell John, though, just for support."

Jenny was soon eliminated from their enquiries, as there was no evidence against her. She still felt ashamed, as she knew her neighbours would have seen her being driven away in a police car. She did tell John and he, as usual, was understanding and supportive. The children nagged her to tell them what the police car ride was like and what happened at the police station. Was she handcuffed? Did they put on the sirens and the blue flashing lights? They were, excitedly, jumping up and down as they asked their mother more questions than the police had done. Jack, their eldest son, was not so enthusiastic. His school mates had heard the story and Jack found it too embarrassing. This was a small village. Why does everyone have to know your business.

Despite her ordeal, her friends were completely sure of Jenny's innocence. Of course, the police now knowing that Jenny was not at home that evening, did not know of John's whereabouts. He was still being investigated.

Chapter 7

"No, I won't wear those things, not to school not ever. You will have to go and buy me the ones I saw in the High Street. If you think I'm wearing these old things you're wrong and you have wasted your money. Gran doesn't even wear shoes like this," protested Angela, in tears, just before the beginning of the new school term.

Angela was a spoilt child. At the age of twelve she dictated the run of the home to her mother. What she wore, what she ate and where they went were all decided by Angela. She was an only child. A beautiful girl. She could get away with murder. Angela's mother had problem pregnancies, all ending in miscarriages before giving birth to her lovely daughter. Angela could also be charming and friendly. She was the it girl at school. Everyone wanted to be her friend and, in spite of her spoilt brat tendencies, she was a good, loyal friend. She stood up to bullies for her friends, she was always a good listener and a magnate to the opposite sex. She knew how attractive she was and could choose any boy she wanted. She flirted with the older boys who were doing their GCSE's. She wasn't interested in boys her own age.

"Mum, I'm off now. See you later," called Angela as she slammed the front door.

"Angela, where are you going? You will have to be back by..." Too late, thought her mother. "Mike, we will really have to be stricter with her. We don't know where she is, who's she's with and when she will be home. She's not even thirteen. Mike, what are we going to do?"

"Don't worry love. She'll be ok, our Angie. She knows what she's doing. She's a sensible lass. She's never late, is she?" Mike Jones was right. The flirting and teasing with the boys that Angela revelled in never became more serious. She did know what she was doing and she made sure she wasn't doing anything other than flirt. Despite her tantrums, she loved her parents and would never hurt them. She just enjoyed the hold she had over her parents, friends and boys. She carried on enjoying life for the rest of her school years.

"I'm not going to sixth form, Mum."

"Why ever not. Your GCSE results were quite good."

"No, I can get a job at Lilley's, on the make-up counter."

"Oh, Angela. Your Dad will be disappointed."

"Look, Mum. A levels and University aren't everything. I'll work my way up. You see, I could be earning loads when my friends are stressing over exams. You'll see, Mum."

Angela persuaded her parents that she was doing the right thing. She did do well at Lilley's, the local department store. She had been there a few years when she met Chris Davies. He came in looking for perfume for his girlfriend.

"Good morning, may I help you."

"Yes please, I don't know what to buy. Perhaps you can help. You will be able to judge a lot better than me."

"Certainly, who is the gift for?"

"It's for my girlfriend. Well, hopefully, my fiancé. I haven't bought the ring, yet but, hope the perfume may be a start and we can choose the ring together."

I have never seen such a gorgeous man, thought Angela as she stood in front of him. She was still able to attract anyone she chose. This was her mission. She was determined that his girlfriend was not going to be his fiancé.

"I am sure I can find you something to please the lady. Let me show you our range."

As Angela walked away she made sure her fingers brushed his hands that were spread out on the counter. Her gesture did not go unnoticed.

"Perhaps, if you don't find what you want today you can call back again. What suits the lady best? What sort does she wear? Is it flowery, fruity, musky? What do you think?"

"I don't know about these things," he laughed.

"I have an idea," said Angela with enthusiasm. "When you have free time, your lunch hour, tomorrow, perhaps?" Angela noted the time and presumed that this was his lunch break. "We could go to the café, here, on the first floor for coffee. I could bring some samples. Try them on me. See what you think."

"Well, I suppose that's an idea. You won't get into trouble for taking the samples out? I want this to be special, though."

"No, I am sure it will lead to a sale. My boss won't mind and I will make sure it's special. It would have to be top of the range, with me going to all this trouble," Angela giggled as she spoke.

"I've put my plan into action, Helen."

"What do you mean, Angela? What plan?"

"You'll see. When he comes in tomorrow I bet you a fiver I will be going out with him within the month."

"Angela, you cow. You're not breaking up his relationship. You can't."

"It won't be my fault. You just wait."

Helen walked away in disgust. She got on well with Angela but, hated the way she used men. She, like other girls was jealous of her ability to get her own way, though. She certainly wasn't going to introduce Angela to her husband.

Angela and Chris started dating. He had become totally smitten by her. He told his girlfriend he didn't think that they were suited. She never received the perfume or, the ring. Angela, who's original idea was to see if she could win him, was now in love with him. She had never felt this way about anyone. Chris was kind, hard working, intelligent and so good looking. It was only six months after they met that she announced her engagement to her parents.

"We're thrilled," shrieked her Mum.

"We are so happy for you both," said Dad as he patted Chris on the shoulder.

They were genuinely pleased that their daughter had found such a decent young man.

Chris had worked hard to pass his exams and, was a practising solicitor by the time that they were married. Angela didn't have to go out to work as Chris earned such a good salary. They moved to a house in Barker's End. This was a new development in a, once, very small village close to Newston. They had decided, before marriage, that they didn't want children. Chris had to work away a lot and, when he was at home they had to entertain a lot of his clients. Neither of them disliked children but, in the back of Angela's mind, she did remember what she was like as a child and this could put any prospective parents off, for good. Angela loved the entertaining and also kept herself busy on village committees.

Angela met her best friend living in Barker's End. After she had left school she didn't have many female friends. Maybe they were all afraid that she would steal their boyfriends. Caroline was the complete opposite of Angela but, they supported each other through the ups and downs of life. Angela was there, after the birth of Caroline's girls, to help in any way she could. They drunk wine together when their husbands were away. Angela really enjoyed her friend's company and was pleased there was, finally, a female friend she could share her life with.

Angela and Caroline both enjoyed walking. The countryside surrounding the village was ideal for this activity. Neither ladies had financial worries so, a pub lunch was always part of the outing. Caroline just had to make sure she was home for the school run.

Angela had the perfect husband, home and life but, it wasn't long before she could see the attractions of the local builder. Paul wasn't from Barker's End. Nobody knew where he was from or anything about him but, for Angela, this led to the attraction. He wasn't charming, good looking or wealthy but, Angela found this a challenge. This was going to be her bit of rough. She approached Paul to do some work on their house but, was mortified when, despite her skilful flirting, he ignored her subtle hints to start an affair, when he called round to give her a quote. I must be old, past it. Why couldn't she get through to this man. They did go out, a few times, for pub lunches away from the village but, in spite a great deal of effort on her part, they never went to bed together.

They didn't expect that it would be Chris's colleague, Ian, who would bump into them one lunchtime. They were at the Merrydown Country club, about twenty miles from Barker's End.

"Oh, Ian, lovely to see you," Angela greeted Ian with embarrassment.

"This is Paul. He is doing some work on the house for us. I know it must seem ridiculous to you that we meet so far from home but, I don't want the neighbours knowing all of our business. You know how it is," Angela's reply was plausible, or so she thought, as she had to think fast. Paul, as usual, didn't say a word.

"Of course," replied Ian. He was not convinced by her story but, he knew, for Chris's sake, that he must keep quiet. It was none of his business.

"He's never going to believe that," said Paul as he sipped his beer.

"Well, there isn't anything going on between us, is there?" replied Angela sarcastically.

Paul handed Angela a box, silently as he carried on drinking.

"Oh, it's lovely, Paul. You are not usually the romantic type."

"It's nothing like that. It's just a thank you for all of the work you put my way. I was going to pay you a sort of commission but, you and your husband have enough money, anyway."

"There are rooms here, you know," laughed Angela as she moved closer to Paul.

"Come on, let's go. I have some quotes to sort out. Some of us have to work for a living."

Angela finished her drink and followed Paul to the car.

"I never thought that I was so unattractive."

"You're not, Angela. You are just not my type."

"Do you have a girlfriend? What is your type?"

"That's my business and not for nosey village gossips to know about." Paul was angry as he pulled onto the main road, spinning the wheels.

Paul hated the way the women of the village behaved. Most of them had too much time on their hands. He wasn't interested in any of them. He had seen, as a child, the effect on families when a woman was unfaithful. He was happy to spend time with Angela. He did enjoy female company but, he just wasn't interested in going to bed with these village tarts.

Angela and Paul drove back to Barker's End in silence. There wasn't a man she couldn't tempt into bed. What was it about him? This was a challenge and she wasn't winning.

Chris and Angela were enjoying dinner, alone, for a change. Chris's anger had been welling up since he arrived home. He put down his knife and fork, almost denting the table.

"Angela why were you with that builder in the Merrydown, last week?" Chris slammed his glass down on the table.

"That's a stupid question. What builder? Why would I be with a builder?"

"I don't know why. That's what I'm asking you. You were seen, so don't lie."

"Who was supposed to see me when I wasn't there?"

"Just stop it. I can't stand it. Don't lie."

Angela never thought that Ian would tell Chris.

"All right. I was there. When did Ian tell you?"

"Ian, what Ian?"

"Your mate, Ian, who you work with, you know, Ian." Angela stopped abruptly. It wasn't Ian.

"If you must know, it was Marcus, that Hilary what's-her-name's husband. What's Ian got to do with it? Are you sleeping with him, as well?"

"Don't be like that, Chris. I'm not sleeping with anyone." Angela was telling the truth.

After Paul was murdered the villagers became suspicious of each other. Everyone suspected everyone else. Even the vicar was not immune to gossip. The murder did bring another man to Angela's attention. James Watson, the young detective who was investigating the crime. He was attractive, in a boyish kind of way. She knew that he was the man her friend was having an affair with. Perhaps she would see if she could attract him. She was sure that she could entice him away from her friend. She had to admit that she was quite jealous of Caroline. She loved Chris and would never leave him but, she was bored.

In spite of the rumours, Angela didn't think that Paul was having affairs with anyone. She had always wondered why Paul was not interested in any of the village women, who offered themselves to him. They were, mostly, attractive, rich women. Angela was even more puzzled and angry when she offered herself to Paul and, he wasn't interested. She was the most attractive and richest of the lot. She presumed he wasn't married. He never mentioned a wife or family. Her conclusion was he must be gay. She, of course, discussed this with her friends and they agreed, this was the reason for his lack of interest in any of them.

During one of Angela's many committee meetings, Yvonne, the secretary of the Women's Institute, said she wanted to meet Angela as she had some interesting news for her, regarding Paul. Angela, keen to know the gossip, agreed that Yvonne should come to her house for a drink, after the meeting. Chris was away and men were not interested in the latest theories about the local builder, anyway.

"Red or white, Yvonne?"

"Red, please, if that's ok? Don't open a bottle especially for me."

"That's fine. Sit down and tell me the news."

"Well, you know Viv, my neighbour, with the baby. Gorgeous little thing. Her husband works away a lot. Anyway, one evening she couldn't get Rosie, that's the baby, to settle. I could hear Rosie screaming, through our bedroom wall. Next thing I heard a car engine. Viv had previously told me that the only way to get Rosie to sleep was a ride in the car."

"Yes but, what has this got to do with Paul?" asked a slightly bored Angela.

"Hang on, I'm coming to that bit. Viv was driving along the lane, that one that goes by the woods. Stupid thing to do, I told her. She said she wasn't scared and loved driving in deserted places. She once told me that she was brought up on a rough council estate and nothing frightened her. Nice girl, not rough at all."

"Yvonne, get to the point. We have got to get to bed sometime tonight."

"Sorry Angela. She saw a couple of men in a parked car. She admitted to being wary as when she drives up the lane she usually sees courting couples, you know boys and girls. She didn't think of gay men. She thought that they may be criminals. You know, robbing farms, something like that. Viv, being a good citizen, writes down the car registration, then drives home as fast as she can. The baby is asleep by then and she is planning on contacting the police with her information. Have you got a drop more red, Angela? This talking is making me thirsty. Lovely wine, this is. The next day Viv takes Rosie to the doctor as she has a temperature and all thoughts of contacting the police are forgotten. Now here's the interesting bit."

"At last," sighs Angela.

"A few days later she is in the supermarket car park when, she sees the car. The criminals car, as she now thinks of them. She gets out the piece of paper, with the registration number on, just to confirm it's the same car. She is on her own as Ryan, her husband is looking after Rosie. She moves her car so, as not to be spotted by the driver and waits for him to return to his car. She slides down in her seat. You know, like they do in those TV dramas. She watches him load his shopping into the car boot. That's strange, she thinks. If he's planning local robberies he wouldn't shop locally, would he? That's not all. She recognises him. He's that builder who does the extensions on the estate. So, what was he doing? The next day she tells me all of this. I put two and two together. I tell Viv that he's not a criminal. He's gay and he was with his boyfriend."

"Well, Yvonne, at last we have the proof. I wonder who his boyfriend is, though, or if he is from this area?"

"Look at the time, Angela. Him indoors will wonder where I am. Thanks for the wine, Bye."

Angela had been proved right. Paul was gay. Probably not cast iron evidence but, enough for Angela and her friends. She was interested to know who the boyfriend was, if he was local.

Angela didn't think of Paul's relationship. She was busy socialising and working on local issues. Angela is an excellent hostess. She has to entertain Chris's clients at least once a month. She, by her own admission, is not the best cook in the world but, she tries hard to please everyone. She always asks Chris if the guests have any allergies or dietary preferences. One day she realises that one of the dinner party guests has allergies. She had remembered his name from previous gatherings. She will have to phone Chris. She never phones him at work but, she has to get this right. Chris is always lunching with him. He will know what she has to buy. She rings Chris's mobile but, hears it ringing in the house. Dam, she thinks. He won't be in the office and his phone is here. She finds the phone on the bedroom floor. It must have fallen out of his pocket. She has an idea. The number of the guest in question, must be stored in the phone. She can phone him herself. She knows all of Chris's contacts. She also knew that he had one night stands. She knew that they meant nothing to him. He was always careful not to call the other women on his mobile or home landline. Whilst scrolling through the names she does come across a name she doesn't recognise. Not a name, just an initial Who's this? She is puzzled by her find. She could just ring it. What if is Chris's latest fling and he has made an error, calling her on his mobile. Angela rings the number but, no reply and no message. She tries a few times but, gives up. This is on her mind but, she mustn't let it distract her. She has a meal to organise. She may never know the who it is. She will leave the phone on the floor and say nothing.

Angela didn't tell Chris that he had left his phone at home. Chris didn't tell Angela that he knew he had. He came home that evening and found the phone on the bedroom floor. Angela wouldn't have had any reason to go into the bedroom. The cleaner made the bed. She came in every morning for an hour. Angela knew that Chris would go straight upstairs to look for his phone. She did tell him that she called him and presumed that he was driving.

A few weeks passed and Angela is still concerned over the phone number. She tells Caroline of her mystery discovery. Angela tries the number on numerous occasions but, no reply. She has to do this surreptitiously. Could she enlist the help of her friends to discover who the mystery person is? Could she drop hints to Chris? She is not going to ask Chris. She is not worried about another women. They have never affected her life style before.

Hilary is having coffee with Angela one morning and discussing the progress of the building extension.

"That Paul may be good at his job but, he has spent most of his time on his mobile, just lately. It's not like him. He usually works non-stop. I think that he has a lover."

"You know that we have found out that he is gay, don't you?"

"Are you sure, Angela? Just because that Viv found him in a car with a man, it doesn't mean that he is gay. They may have been discussing dodgy business and that's why it was in the dark down a country lane. Although, I'm sure his calls are from his lover. He doesn't seem to have any friends and family and always takes business calls without rushing outside. Another thing. He has got two mobiles. When he rushed to take a secret call, for about the tenth time, I was putting a cup of tea on the worktop, when I saw a mobile. I knew it wasn't mine so, realised our friendly, or not so friendly, builder has a secret phone."

"Well, if he is running a business he probably needs another phone for private use," replied a reasonable Angela.

"Yes, ok but, we all know that he doesn't have a private life. He now spends more time chatting than building and I'm paying him. It must be a new lover," said an indignant Hilary.

Hilary was still keen to find out more about Paul's private life. Perhaps the next time he visits the suppliers he may leave the secret phone behind.

Hilary never did find out the identity of the caller but, Angela did. Paul and Angela were having one of their lunches out when he took a call. He went into the pub garden looking agitated. Angela, like Hilary, knew that Paul always took his business calls openly. He had nothing to hide regarding his business deals. This must be his secret phone.

"Who's that? You look very furtive. Your latest fling?"

"No, just a customer."

"Come off it, Paul. You blushed as you, literally, ran out of the pub."

"None of your business."

"No, just being friendly."

"Well, don't."

This made Angela all the more curious. She must find out. All of the girls would want to know. Paul's love life was talk of the girl's get togethers. They were all determined to find out who his mystery lover was. Angela enjoyed her lunches with Paul. She may not have been able to get him into bed and it now looks as if he had a new distraction. He did talk to her. He never mentioned his private life but, in a strange way they were friends.

It was Viv, the discoverer of Paul's sexuality, that was to help solve the mystery of the phone calls. She was out in the village when she heard a telephone conversation well, one side of it. She didn't mean to listen. She'd gone to look for Rosie's toy rabbit. She knew that it had fallen out of the pushchair when she had left the paper shop. At the side of the shop was an alleyway. She could see down the passage, that led to the churchyard. There it was. A pink, fluffy object. It must have got kicked down the alleyway. Probably kids using it as a football. As she approached the fluffy toy she could hear a voice. She couldn't see anyone but, the conversation seemed heated. He must be around the corner, in the churchyard. She could only make out that it was a man. She picked up the rabbit and stayed as still as possible. She was glad that Rosie was with her Mum. Rosie wouldn't have stayed silent in that alleyway. She just heard these words.

"Chris, we can't leave yet. I've got to finish the job I'm working on. Just a few more days and we'll be together, forever."

Viv didn't have a clue who it was. She just knew it was a man's voice. How could she find out? Perhaps she could run around to the High Street, walk through the church yard and he may still be there. She put her plan into action but, he was gone. The church yard was empty but, the church wasn't. She could still hear the voice. She must try and see who it was. She would hide behind a gravestone and wait for him to come out. She didn't have to hurry home. This was fun. A pleasant change from child care. How long would she have to hide, though? What if someone walked by? Everyone knew everyone else in this village. They would ask her what she was doing. Even if they didn't speak, the whole village would know that Viv has got enough to do with a young child but, still finds time to hide behind gravestones. When he came out of the church she recognised him. It's that builder again, the one in the car. She must have been mistaken that evening when she saw him in the lane. He was leaving with a girl. A girl called Chris. Christine, a girl.

Viv told her neighbour, Yvonne, what she had witnessed. She said that she felt a fool and Paul must have been with a girl that night or, just meeting a man for a dodgy deal.

"Not, necessarily," said Yvonne. Chris could be a man."

"Why didn't I think of that. Chris, Christopher. We were right and he is leaving with his lover."

Yvonne, excitedly, told Angela. She telephoned her has soon as she left Viv.

"Detective Viv has come up trumps, again."

"He's leaving?"

"Yes, with someone called Chris, male or female."

"Well, now we know. Your Viv is certainly useful."

"Yes, she is."

Angela had to reward this useful young woman.

"Hello, Yvonne. I was thinking of that young Viv, your neighbour. I suppose that she doesn't get out much. Well, you know she takes out her little girl,

Rosie, isn't it? She can't have a lot of time to herself. Has she friends in the village?"

"Oh, hello, Angela. Why do you ask about Viv? I don't know who her friends are but, she does seem to spend a lot of time just with Rosie. Of course, I invite her round for coffee but, she probably thinks that I am just an old busy body, fuddy duddy. I know that her parents visit at the weekend but, her Mum still works. They live in Newston. So do her in-laws."

"It's just that I thought that I might invite her to our next coffee morning. What do you think?"

"That's a lovely idea, Angela. She is a shy girl but, I hope that we can make her feel welcome."

"I will just go and knock on her door. Might as well get the ball rolling."

Viv was not part of Angela's estate set. Yvonne new this but, appreciated Angela being kind to her young neighbour. Yvonne never thought that she was part of Angela's set but, she did enjoy the gossip with the other woman.

"Ryan, I am not sure that I should be going to that coffee morning. She's very posh, you know, that Angela. It's very nice of her to invite me. Her friends are posh as well. Why does she want me there?"

"Viv, just go. She won't eat you. You won't be on your own, anyway. Yvonne will be with you. You never know, you might enjoy it." Ryan kissed her forehead as he left for work.

Of course, she would go. She wouldn't let Yvonne down. She could make new friends. Extra baby sitters, she giggled to herself.

"Are you all set, Viv? We might as well walk to Angela's together."

"I'm ready, Yvonne but, there is just one thing. I will have to bring Rosie with me. Will Angela mind? She doesn't seem the type to me to want toddlers crawling all over her furniture. In fact, she doesn't seem the type to want me in her house. She hasn't got children, has she?"

"Oh, don't worry about that. I told her that you might bring Rosie along. Most of Angela's friends have children. She will adore Rosie. So will the other girls. Come along. Just relax. You will enjoy yourself and will have me to hold your hand," chuckled Yvonne as she helped to get the pushchair out of the house.

"I didn't have to make a cake, did I? I just didn't think."

"No, no dear. Angela is a fantastic cook, even if she doesn't think so, herself. All those dinner parties that her and Chris have. I even told her what your favourite was."

Viv did enjoy herself at the coffee morning. She didn't have to worry about Rosie. She hardly saw her daughter. The other ladies had taken it in turns to keep her amused and feed her cake. Never mind, thought Viv. It is not often that her daughter gets spoilt.

"Viv, try this cherry cake. A little bird told me that it is your favourite and I've been told that you make a rather good one yourself."

"I do love a cherry cake but, I'm not sure mine would be half as good as yours."

"You haven't tried it yet," laughed Angela.

"Angela, did you put fresh cherries in this? I use those sticky, sweet things that you buy in tubs."

"Yes, I did put fresh one's in this one. I usually do, if I can get them."

"Yvonne said you were a good cook."

"Go on, have some more. It's not as though you have to be on a diet, like most of us."

Viv walked home with Yvonne and her sleeping, over fed daughter.

"Do you think that she will invite me again? I did enjoy the company. Everyone is so friendly. Angela's house is like one of those I read about in magazines."

"I'm sure that this will be a regular event. I have to say that Rosie was a very popular guest."

"I know, Yvonne. I am just Rosie's Mum. I was a person, you know."

The women parted with a cheerful goodbye.

"I did really enjoy the coffee morning, although, I must admit, I didn't expect too."

"That's good, Viv, because I could tell that the girls enjoyed your company. It wasn't just Rosie That they were interested in, you know. You're not just Rosie's Mum. You're an interesting woman. I didn't know that you are a proper scientist."

Viv felt her confidence rise, as her friend, Yvonne, spoke to her. She felt she was now a woman, in her own right.

"Anyway, as there are many of Angela's monthly events, I am sure you will be invited to something. The next coffee morning, I'm sure of. Perhaps you would consider joining the Women's Institute, with me. If you want to, of course. You don't want too much of a good thing," Yvonne laughed.

"I'll see. I don't want to get involved in evening events. Ryan has a lot of travelling to do. I don't want him to have to do a lot of child care when he gets home. He might even miss me if I am gadding about every evening. He'd be quite happy to look after Rose all day. He helps a lot at the week-end," Viv considered her reply to her helpful friend.

Viv didn't have to wait for the next coffee morning to see Angela.

"Oh, good morning, come in. I wasn't expecting anyone. I don't get many visitors, except Yvonne. She pops in a lot."

"I know how much you enjoyed my cherry cake so, I thought that I would make one just for you. Really, as a thank you for coming the other day, and of course, bringing your charming daughter. You are the only girl I know that doesn't need to diet so, you see my cakes will only go to waste, if you don't eat them. We are all jealous of you."

"Thank you, Angela. I don't know what to say."

"Don't say anything. Put the kettle on and we will have a slice. At least you will have a slice. I really must be good. I have just brought this gorgeous dress for this do. I am going with Chris and any extra calories will show as a bulge. I'm on a crash diet until Friday. Then, it will all be over and I can eat a bit more."

"Oh, Angela, you haven't got an ounce of fat on you. If it means I have to eat it all, I will. Ryan doesn't like cake. I don't let Rosie eat it as she is a little bit podgy. Yvonne is on a permanent diet. Ah well, I will have to manage," she laughed.

Angela had gone out with Paul for one of their lunches. Chris seemed to accept that there was nothing but friendship between them. She asked Paul when he was leaving.

"What, how did you know? When did you find out? Did he tell you? I thought we would wait until I was ready. You're pretty calm about it, my God I've never met a woman like you."

"Calm, why shouldn't I be calm. You and me we're just friends. Not even friends, really. Why should I care if you're leaving? The girls will miss you're building skills and, they did find you attractive, in a funny kind of way. I'm glad that you have find someone. It might cheer you up. Wait, calm, Chris, P," Angela's voice trailed off as she realised she had solved the puzzle.

"Shit, you didn't know. I thought that you had found out."

"I know now, thank you. Why didn't I work it out. Chris, P. Why didn't I think. He's not gay." Angela was now crying hysterically.

Angela sat waiting for her husband to return from work. She had composed herself. She was very calm, she thought, under the circumstances. She was determined not to cry in front of Chris. She didn't need him. She was strong and she could cope. Even Caroline was not going to know about this, yet. Chris didn't even deny it. He told her everything. She sat in silence as her world, the life she knew, and everything she had ever wanted, started to collapse. She must get through this. The next day she continued to carry on as though nothing had happened. Chris was away but, she would have to talk to Paul. Make him see sense.

"Good morning, Mrs Davies. May we come in and have a quick word. We are here in connection with the murder of Mr. Robertson."

"Please, do come in. Would you like tea, coffee?"

"No thank you, Mrs Davies, this shouldn't take too long," answers Detective Sergeant Emma Dunn, as she sits herself down on Angela's cream sofa. Her colleague, WPC Julie Morris, stands by the window.

"How can I help you," asks Angela.

Caroline is standing against the worktop in Angela's kitchen listening to the conversation taking place in the next room. She is surprised by Angela's reaction to the questions from the police. Cool, calm, in-control Angela seems a little un-nerved.

"Mrs Davies, the locals have told us that you partake in a lot of village activities, fund raising, that sort of thing. We are led to believe that if any rumours are spread locally that you would be the first to know." We have reason to believe that Mr Roberston was in a relationship with a local woman. Have you heard anything that might substantiate this rumour?"

Angela is staring in the direction of Caroline, through the kitchen doorway. Her voice and expression concern Caroline.

"No, sorry, I wasn't aware that Paul was seeing anyone. No, not as far as I know. It's probably just gossip. You know what these communities are like. I didn't know much about him, though. I wouldn't know of his personal life. I don't know why anyone should think I know anything about him."

This defensive, serious manner is very unusual for Angela. What has upset her? What does she know about Paul?

"Thank you, anyway, Mrs Davies. We will see ourselves out."

"Angela, are you ok?" asks a concerned Caroline as she comes in from the kitchen, gripping her mug of tea. "I've never seen you look nervous, not even in the presence of the police. I just stutter and mumble at the sight of the uniform, even if I am driving quite innocently along the road." Caroline sits by her friend on the sofa.

"Of course, I'm all right. You know me. I think my period must be due. You know how it is. I'm tired, have a headache and can't think straight. That's all."

"Yes, that'll be it." You always did suffer bad with PMT. I'll go now, got housewife things to do. You know, cleaning the toilet. The jobs us ladies do best," replied Caroline, still un-convinced by her friends reply.

Did Angela know Paul better than she led anyone to believe? Does she know the woman he was having an affair with? These thoughts whirled round in Caroline's head as she walked home. Why was her friend holding evidence from the police? Was she protecting another friend? A married friend who was involved with Paul.

Caroline found her friends behaviour unusual when the police questioned her. It was still on her mind when Nick came in.

"You know I still don't understand why she met Paul alone to discuss the extension. Chris has a say in all the major decisions," Nick listened to Caroline's account of Angela's meeting with Paul.

"Chris is away, a lot. This time he could have thought that he would leave it up to Angela. Perhaps he had too much on at work to worry about the house. You know Angela likes to take control. This time he may have just let her."

Nick finally agreed with his wife as he poured her a cup of tea.

Caroline was not convinced. Was Angela having an affair with Paul?

Chapter 8

Barker's End is a typical English village. It's the type of place that tourists think of when they think of England. Cottages with neat gardens, Wisteria growing up the walls. Thatched roofs and a village green. Ducks roaming around the pond, waiting for some kind child to throw a crust of bread. The church bells ringing and, the trees decorated with pink blossom in spring. The village is situated five miles from the town of Newston, which is not what tourists think of or, even visit. Newston has no attractive features. It doesn't have historical buildings, beautiful parks or much entertainment. It was built as a new town after the war. Housing people was the priority. There is a cinema, pubs and two nightclubs. These venues keep the locals amused at the week-ends. In spite of its lack of beauty the residents say it is a friendly place and they wouldn't live anywhere else. There is no railway station so, most of the residents travel by bus or car to work in nearby larger towns. There is some industry and well known chain stores provide employment and shopping facilities in the high street. The locals are mainly retired and have lived here for most of their lives. The families with children do manage to populate the secondary school and the older teenagers keep the night time economy going.

Barker's End is full of antique shops, cafes and restaurants which the tourists need after the photo stops. The old village, whereby old translates to people who were born and bred in the village and, live on the farms or in the picturesque cottages. There is a road dominated by local authority houses. The village also has a school, pub, church, post office and church hall. It is a pleasant place to live and, a lot of the villagers commute by car to nearby towns.

The old residents will tell you that Barker's End was a better place to live before they decided to build on Rowans farm. Old Ted had farmed Rowans for years, with his father and grandfather before him. After he died his family knew that the developers were keen to build on the land. Ted's daughters couldn't resist the sum of money being offered to them. The deal was sealed, planning permission granted and the new estate was built. Despite objections, by the locals, that there wasn't any work for the new residents. Their concerns were quickly shot down, as they were told the owners would be professional people all working from home, travelling to meetings, when required. The show house had a purpose built office. Living in a picturesque village was the attraction. Not to mention, an excellent Ofsted report for the local primary school.

As with many new developments, you could not convince people that it was a good idea.

There were a number of plus points which the housing estate brought to Barker's End. The primary school would have closed if not for its many more new pupils. The shop, pub and post office had many more customers. Even the vicar was pleased with his enlarged Sunday congregation.

A few years after the estate was built most of the old villagers could see the benefit. The centre was livelier. The new people did, generally, want to join in with village life. Some of the local tradesman, such as John Gilbert, the carpenter, could see the work these wealthy people would bring. The estate was for wealthy people. Posh people on the estate, they were known as. The village women didn't really mix with the new ladies. Too posh, they thought. The men were better integrated. Pub, football, cricket: It didn't matter how much money you had, these were common interests. The children mixed well as they attended the village school or, Newston Community College.

Viv was one of the newcomers but, was not at all posh. This was confirmed by her husband, Ryan.

"Hi, love. I'm just making a cherry cake for the bring and buy sale. You know, the one in the village hall, on Saturday. I think I'll make a couple of buns with the left over mixture. I love them."

"Viv, you keep them to yourself and don't bring that cake back. I hate that cherry cake. I think it's those horrible, sweet cherry things that go into it. I know it's your weakness and it doesn't spoil your lovely figure, so you eat as many of those buns as you like, said Ryan, as he kissed her on the top of her head. Her hands and mind were occupied with a basin and a wooden spoon.

"Look at this. Who would have thought that clever research scientist would be at home in the kitchen?"

"I think that the saying is, baking is a science and cooking is an art, or the other way round, you know," laughed Viv.

Viv and Ryan moved into the new estate in Barker's End with their new baby. They were not the usual, middle class type of resident that the estate was used too. In fact, Ryan said, he was a typical working class lad. Ryan was a heating engineer. He had a large area of the country to cover but, he loved his job. He loved his wife and daughter even more. He was a happy man. Ryan and Viv would have never been able to afford a house in Barker's End. They couldn't afford a house, anywhere. Not even a shed, as Viv used to tell her friends. They had both been fortunate in being only grandchildren of proud grandparents. They both inherited a very large sum of money when their respective grandmothers died. Both grandads had passed away a few years before.

Viv and Ryan were very happy. Not, of course, at losing their grandmothers but, they were going to be free of a mortgage and they were in love. They had met at school when they were both thirteen years old. It was love at first sight. Everyone said that it wouldn't last. They were far too young. They would have other relationships. They didn't. They still had that first love sparkle as they had when they walked home from school together.

Viv was taking the opportunity to make a pie, while her daughter slept. She was chatting to her mother while she cooked.

"Mum, I'm not going back to work. I'm not a career girl, like you."

"Viv, I'd hardly say I was a career girl. I'm just a small cog, who is far too old for promotion, in a very large accounts office. I do love my job, the company, being out of the house and the money. You are such a clever girl, Viv. You could go a long way in that research institute."

"Yes, yes, I know, Mum. I'm not like you. I want to be a full time mother and housewife. I love cooking, looking after Rosie, cleaning. I know that's alien to you. Gardening, walking round the village. I will never get fed up with it. If I do, in years to come, I will get a job."

"Thanks, Viv. Are you saying that you grew up in a filthy hovel?" her Mum laughed as she reprimanded her daughter.

"You know I'm not, Mum. You kept the house lovely. You brought me up, cooked and kept Dad happy. All of that and a job. It's just not for me."

"Well, if you're sure. You won't get such a good job, though. You'll forget all that science stuff you have learnt at University."

"I know. I'll just have to take that risk. Ryan has a good job. This is really what I want. I've already made a good friend in Yvonne, next door. The other girls are not really my type but, I've made friends in the village. I'm so happy. I can't believe it."

Ryan arrived home early one evening to receive the shock of his life.

Bill and Jim were neighbours who both lived in the houses that they were born in. There were the original old villages and had never got used to the newcomers. They were discussing the devastating news that was now common knowledge in the village.

"I suppose you've heard about that terrible business, Jim. That poor young girl. Killed herself. She's got that little kiddie, as well. Why would she want to do that?"

"You're right, Bill. Her husband found her when he came home from work. You just can't imagine what he's going through. Her Mum and Dad, as well. Lost a lovely daughter. The only thing, and you can't say it's a good thing but, perhaps a blessing, is that the child may be too young to understand and remember."

"You know my girl, Sue. You know her Jim, course you do. Well, her friend knows the receptionist at the doctors. They heard from the police. Well, they say she killed herself with cyanide."

"Cyanide, what do you mean? You can't buy that now. You could only get that years ago, from chemists, I think. That was even before our time. They must have got that wrong."

"Well, I am only telling you what I have been told."

Caroline had been upset by both the recent local deaths.

"Angela, I really can't get over another death. This is such a peaceful village. How can Paul be murdered after poor Viv died?" Caroline was pulling her soggy tissue apart, as she spoke.

"Caroline, this is still a peaceful village. Viv and Paul's death are not related. Viv committed suicide. This does sometimes happen in communities. Just a succession of tragedies. No, I'm getting as bad as you. Not a succession. It is two unconnected deaths."

"There was a lady killed here, twenty five years ago and, they never caught her killer."

"Yes, I know but, the opinion was, it was her husband. The police will look into this, of course. They will want to know if there is a strange serial killer that only operates every twenty odd years. It's crazy, I know. Viv has nothing to do with this. She may have been suffering from post natal depression."

"What? Her daughter wasn't a tiny baby."

"No, I know but, you never know. She was stuck all day with a small child. Look, I don't know but, the verdict was suicide."

"Viv came to your coffee mornings. She loved your cake. She seemed happy to be accepted by the other women. Everyone adored Rosie." Caroline was sobbing as she spoke.

"Caroline, people are very good at hiding their feelings. That's the problem."

Ryan had asked the police to get involved, as he wasn't happy with the verdict that his wife had committed suicide.

"I can't believe that she would kill herself, Inspector, sorry Chief Inspector. I know it can't be true. They say that you don't always know if someone is depressed. I would know. I know the signs. My mother suffered from depression, all the time when I was a child. I could tell when she was going through her dark times, as my Dad called it. She did get help and is fine now, apart from odd occasions. Viv slept, ate ok. We had a good, you know what I mean, a close relationship. You know, sex and all that. She looked after the house and Rosie and had just made some new friends in the village. I thought, well we both did, that they were a bit posh but, they seemed to take to her and Rosie. She didn't kill herself, Inspector, um Chief Inspector. That's why I wanted the police involved. Bye the way, just call me Ryan. None of this Mr. stuff."

"Ryan, I tend to agree with you. I think that your wife's death was suspicious. I will ask some questions, starting with your neighbour," Alan Stock left Ryan's house in no doubt that this grieving widower was right.

"Good morning, Mrs."

"Oh, Yvonne, please. No one calls me Mrs. I'm old enough as it is. That just makes me feel older."

"Yvonne, we are here about your neighbour. We need to ask you a few questions."

"Poor Viv, she just didn't seem the sort to kill herself. Is there a sort? I suppose not. Poor Ryan. What is Rosie going to do? I just don't understand it. Of course, I will look after Rosie, but."

"Mrs, Yvonne, the report suggests that Viv was killed by cyanide. You were very close to your neighbour. Very helpful and supportive, according to other residents. Do you know where she would be able to obtain cyanide?"

"Cyanide. That's what they used in the olden days. You know, the Dickens stories. Serial killers. They seemed to get it easily, them days, from the chemist. I don't think that our chemist would stock it. Do you? I think they must be wrong, don't you? Well, you'll never believe this. What a coincidence. Do you know? Well, of course you don't. I'm rambling. I always do that. Viv's terrible death has made me worse. Anxious, nervous, you understand? Back to the coincidence. My friend, can't remember who but, never mind, gave me a magazine the other week. What's this got to do with Viv, you ask. Well these women's magazines they have these short stories. You ask your wife. You won't know, Inspector. They won't appeal to you. This particular story was about an old lady who found out that her carer was trying to kill her, for her money. Anyway, the old lady had found out. I forget that bit, how she found out. She found out that if you grind up cherry stones, and it doesn't take many, that you can kill someone. Apparently, they turn into cyanide in your body and you can't taste them. Of course, I had to look on the internet to see if this was true. It is. Rather a good story I thought. Poetic justice and all that. Don't take notice of me. Just it's a coincidence."

"Thank you, Mrs, Yvonne. We may need to speak to you again."

Ryan had told the police that Yvonne was a lovely lady. The best neighbour that anyone could have.

"She is always cheerful, helpful and friendly. Viv is, oh, I can't bring myself to say it, was, always grateful for her help and advice. Yvonne's own sons were away at University. She always knew what to do if Viv had a problem or worry over Rosie. Viv's Mum and my Mum were brilliant grannies but, they were at work all day. Yvonne ran a business at home. She never seemed to be that busy, though. I haven't a clue what she does. Her one fault was that she talked too much. Goes off on a tangent. You know what I mean. My Mum does it."

"Yes, I know exactly what you mean," said DCI Stock, rubbing his chin. Deep in thought.

Everyone in the village agreed that Yvonne was a lovely, bubbly lady. A lot of them were irritated that it took her so long to get to the point. He had forgotten what the subject was by the time she had finished. They all told the police that Yvonne would never hurt anyone, especially young Viv. She was the daughter she never had.

Alan Stock had always thought that the nosey woman theories, a part portrayed by Miss Marple, was too quick to be dismissed by many of his colleagues. If you listened carefully you would, usually, find that what they had to say was relevant. He had spent a life time interviewing these women. They knew everything about everybody. This was real police work. Taking notice of people who knew. If only Yvonne could remember who gave her that magazine. If Viv's death wasn't suicide, Yvonne has put herself under suspicion.

Angela had to tell Chris the horrible news, before he went out.

"Chris, have you heard?"

"I don't know, Angela. Heard what?"

"Viv, you know, Viv. The young Mum who has been coming to my coffee mornings."

"Well. You know that I don't know all of your friends but, what about her?"

"She committed suicide. I can't believe it. She is, was so sweet and had a lovely little girl. Why would she do that?"

"Perhaps she had marriage problems. Did you meet her husband?"

"No, no but, I'm sure that they were happy. How awful for him and the baby. Perhaps I should go and see him. What do I say?" Yvonne says that they were a lovely, happy, little family."

"Well, if Yvonne says so, then it must be true."

"Chris, this is no time to joke."

"I know but, we can't bring her back. You must do what you think best, love." Chris kisses Angela on the cheek before he leaves for work.

Now another death has shocked the village. When Paul Robertson was murdered the new residents were to blame, according to the old village.

"Well, he wouldn't have been here, for a start," said Jim to his neighbour. "He only came here to work on them houses, in the first place."

"Yes, yes, true enough, Jim. We never had anything like this happen before that estate was built."

"I told you, it would bring nothing but trouble. They think that young woman was murdered now, you know. There are very suspicious goings on, here. Look at the vicar and that other chap. You know him who works, if that's what you call it, on the hall. You know him. Does a bit in the graveyard."

"Yes, Jim. I know who you mean but, he's not really a local. Is he? I know he doesn't live on the estate but, he hasn't been here long."

"No, a funny bloke, if you ask me. Betty told me and, she heard it in the post office, that when the vicar and that other one was interviewed by the police, they both acted suspiciously."

"The vicar wouldn't murder anyone, surely?"

"No, he wouldn't but, I wouldn't put it past that strange helper of his. And you know Keith, in the pub. Well, he's a nervous wreck now that the police are always here."

"Well, he's always been a funny chap but, he's not a murderer, Jim."

"I know Bill, I know. I'm not saying anyone in the village is a murderer. I just think that it is strange this should happen a few years after that new lot arrived. If you ask me, my monies on one of them posh blokes. He found out that his wife was having an affair with that murdered builder. My Betty has heard some tales of what goes on when he is working on them houses."

"It's not the first murder we've had in the village. Is it Bill?"

"No, you're right, Jim, and that were never solved. It can't be the same killer, surely. The new houses weren't even thought of, then."

"Well, must go in for dinner, now, Jim. No doubt we'll find out soon enough."

"Cheerio, Bill."

Christine Jackson's body was found, on the road to Newston, twenty five years ago. She was discovered in a ditch by the vicar. Christine was a local farmer's wife. Bob Jackson, her husband, was arrested for the murder. He was re-arrested many times but, no evidence could be found and he was never charged. The murder was never solved even though the locals were convinced that Bob was the killer. He became ostracised from the village. He carried on, working, alone. He later sold the farm and moved to Australia. Alan Stock, the DCI, would be failing in his duty if he did not look into the possibly connection of the two murders.

Christine Jackson was known in the village but, didn't socialize with anyone in particular. She was friendly and pleasant when she encountered anyone. She would chat to shop keepers and the vicar. When asked if she would come to church, attend coffee mornings or any other village get togethers, she would always, cheerfully, decline and say that she was far too busy. The truth was that she was far too busy. Bob and Christine ran a large farm by themselves. They didn't employ farm labourers so, every animal and every crop that was grown had to be looked after by the Jacksons. Christine never complained. She always seemed happy and healthy.

When Bob was arrested for Christine's murder the villagers were stunned. Why would he murder the woman that he loved? Why would he destroy his working partnership and get rid of his unpaid help? The business was doing well. He wouldn't benefit from his wife's death. She came from a working-class family in the village. Bob was the only possible suspect. They didn't socialise but, they didn't have enemies. Christine's parents had both died when she was in her twenties. Bob's mother and father had retired to the coast. They had given the farm to Bob, as he was their only child. They had no motive to harm their daughter-in-law. Their son was happily married, and Christine was an asset to his business.

Some villagers were always suspicious of the new vicar. He found the body and rumours had spread that he and Christine were having an affair. There was no evidence to substantiate the gossip. A few women in Barker's End said that Christine sparkled when she was near the vicar. They said that she changed from her farm dungarees to pretty dresses if she thought that there was a chance that she might bump into the vicar. It was rumoured that she knew the days and times that he would be at the Post Office or, the village store. The same vicar is still in Barker's End and is a popular man.

DCI Stock still doesn't know why the vicar is uneasy when the police are near but, he will do what he can to eliminate him from being a suspect in a twenty five year old unsolved murder or, current suspicious deaths. I know when someone isn't a murderer, he thought to himself.

The common opinion on the subject of Paul Robertson's murder was, it wouldn't have happened if the new estate hadn't have been built.

"I've got something to tell you, Bill. I was taking Benjy for his nightly outing and I saw ...You know what is that young girl's name?"

"What girl are you talking about?"

"She's married to the carpenter. Their families both live in the village. I've known them both since they were little uns. Nice little kiddies, they were. I think that they have got four or five of their own, now."

"Oh, Jenny, you mean. What about her?"

"Well, as I said, I was taking Benjy out. You know how he has got used to going out late. I don't know why I ever started that. A bad habit I got him into. Now he'll whine all night, if I don't take him out at midnight. It's as though he can tell the time. Anyway, she didn't see me, so I didn't speak. I didn't want to frighten her in the middle of the night. I never, usually, see a soul at that time. I wonder what she was doing."

"Perhaps she couldn't sleep. She grew up here and feels safe walking about all hours."

"She may have felt safe but, now we have murderers on the loose. Anyway, it was the night that that chap got murdered. I had to tell the police I saw her. I had to do my duty. Some folks round here think that her and her husband wanted him out the way. He was taking his work. They wouldn't kill him, though, would they."

"Keep your doors and windows locked, Jim. I'm not going out after dark and not answering the door to anyone. We have a serial killer on the loose."

"Bye, Bill. See you later."

Angela had other things on her mind. Unlike Caroline, her friend, the village tragedies were not her worries.

"Chris, you ought to see Hilary's new extension. It puts ours in the shade, a bit."

"I'm sure we'll see it, soon enough, Angela."

"It's just that everything seems to fit, so perfect in the new room."

"I thought that you told me that it was just going to be used as a playroom."

"Well, it is, but, all of the cupboards and drawers look, well, just right in a pink and grey colour scheme."

"We don't need a playroom. We chose not to have children. Remember? Marcus probably earns a lot more than me or, at least he has Mummy and Daddy to bail him out. We haven't got that luxury to fall back on. Angela, I thought that you were happy with our home, life, etc."

"I am Chris, don't take any notice of me. Our house is lovely and no children to mess it up."

"Anyway, must dash, and don't you go asking that Paul chap to do any alterations whilst I'm away."

Chris kissed Angela on the cheek, picked up his bag and hurried out of the door. Later that day, Angela went to see her friend.

"Caroline, have you seen Hilary's house?"

"Angela, you know that Hilary and I are not best friends. Why would she invite me in to show me her new extension?"

"Oh, no reason. Paul does make a good job of things, though. You're not into all that, are you?"

"What do you mean, not into all that? Are you saying that my house is a tip?" Caroline laughed as she poured her friend a cup of tea.

"Your home is spotless. I don't know how you do it with two little ones. It's just that you are not materialistic like the rest of us. That's what I like about you. You're different."

"I can't afford to be. The girls take any spare cash for shoes, clothes, annual trip to the coast, for a week, everything. I didn't grow up with rich parents, so I never expected much. If I wanted extras I could go out to work but, I'd rather not."

"No, I understand. Hilary and Marcus have children but, his parents do own a business. Have you ever wondered about Hilary, though?"

"No, not really. You know that I don't like her because she thinks that she is better than me."

"I'm supposed to be her friend but, I know nothing about her. She doesn't seem to have any family, at all."

"Well, you are much more likely to know about her life than me. Why the sudden interest?"

"I don't know. It's just that she didn't really want Paul to work on the house. He has done a brilliant job but, she says that she wouldn't use him again. Perhaps it's a cover up. They could be having an affair."

"There again, she is much more likely to confide in you, than anyone else."

"Yes, I know. Just thinking aloud."

"Well, stop thinking and drink your tea."

Later that day, the Mums were gossiping in the school playground.

"You know what I think, don't you?"

"No, Jackie, I don't know what you think."

"I think that Hilary could have killed Paul, that builder chap."

"Why, whatever makes you think that?"

"I think that her and Paul were having an affair. Everyone says that she didn't really want him in the house. I bet that was because they were seeing each other. She probably ended the affair. I can't see her wanting to give up her cosy life with Marcus. She wouldn't want to be with Paul. Perhaps he didn't want to end it so, she had to get rid of him."

"Well, I do get your reasoning but, I am sure that Hilary is not a murderer."

"We will have to wait and see. I am sure that the police are looking into every relationship that Paul may, or may not, have had."

Keith was having his usual lunch time drink with his friends. The pub was never busy at that time of day. To be honest, it wasn't that busy any time of day. It ticked over, as he would say to Kath. When there was a darts tournament or a cricket match he made enough money to last for weeks.

"Why don't you two just calm down," said Keith, speaking firmly, in a low voice, as he spoke to his drinking guests.

"I know that the police are onto us," replied the vicar, lifting his pint, his eyes darting nervously, around the bar.

"What are you talking about? The police are investigating a murder and, possibly a suspicious death in this village. Did you kill either of the victims?"

"No, no, of course I didn't. What do you mean suspicious death? That young woman with the baby. I thought they said it was suicide. Was she murdered, as well? I get very edgy and tongue tied when they question me."

"Well don't. Just keep calm."

"How about you?" Keith addressed the quiet church handyman. "You're not saying much."

"I don't like it either, Keith. They came to see me about this murder business."

"Are you the murderer?"

"Don't talk daft, Keith."

"Well then. Both of you keep calm. If you want, we can stop for a while, until this is all over."

"That's ok for you to say that, Keith. I've got all the stuff in the loft in the church hall."

"Well, if you can't cope, bring it to me."

"No, someone might see us. Everyone is watching everyone else in this village. They will see me shifting the stuff."

"Just leave things as they are then and act normal. If you pair can do that. Oh, watch out. Here comes trouble. Change the subject."

The three men took a sip of their beer and discussed who was going to win the premier league, as Keith's wife entered the bar to greet them.

Chapter 9

Detective Chief Inspector Alan Stock saw a lot of himself in young Watson. The enthusiasm was there, at the beginning, for himself, just as it was for James Watson. No, it's wrong to say it was there. It still is for Alan. He has just changed, with old age.

Alan Stock knew that he wanted to be a policeman. His father, his uncle and his grandfather had all joined the police force. His mother wasn't happy with his career choice. She was always scared of the increasing violence, as she saw it, in today's world. Alan's brother worked on the railways. A much safer occupation, in his mum's opinion.

"Not so sure about that." Alan used to tease his mother. "Pete goes out and inspects those tracks. What if someone forgets to stop the oncoming trains?" He would question his mum with a hint of mischief.

"Don't be daft, you. The railways know what to do. Safety is their first concern. You will never know what you are up against." His mother always had that hint of despair in her voice whenever she spoke of Alan's job.

"I'll be ok Mum, Trust me."

Alan Stock was one of those fortunate people who always was ok. This was really down to his character. He never wanted to be an action man. He wasn't going to join the Sweeney, racing around with blue lights and sirens. He would be like his Dad. He could talk himself out of, or into, trouble.

At eighteen years of age Alan started his dream job and was enrolled at the police training college. He, by his own admission, made a lot of mistakes, when he was first let loose on the public. He soon gained respect amongst the public, his colleagues and even, the local criminals. His approach had always been the same. Try to talk to them. This had worked especially well on first time and young offenders. No heroic actions or violence, from him, anyway. Of course, he had some difficult customers. He had seen some upsetting situations but, he knew what to expect and it didn't affect his private life.

Alan Stock married Jill. She knew what she was letting herself in for and accepted his career. He never let work interfere with his home life. He, unlike some of his colleagues, never needed the help of a drink to cope. Well, that is if you don't include the tea. Alan loved his tea. As much as he tried, he couldn't cut down. Not even on the three sugars.

It was the respect of everyone, including his bosses, that earned him promotions. He had an ability to solve crimes quietly, without theatricals, as he would say.

Alan Stock had grown up, and still lived in a town. He could never see the appeal of village life. Working in Barker's End had done nothing to change his opinion. Everyone knew everyone else's business. They all knew what each other were doing. How anyone got away with an affair, he couldn't see. As for murder. It's a surprise that there were no witnesses, even if it was in the middle of the night. Was there a witness? Is someone protecting the murderer? Alan Stock is good at solving crimes. It's what he has always done. This one doesn't make sense. He must look at all of the facts.

Alan had his main suspects, in his mind. Apart from them, a lot of other residents seemed to have something to hide. He was convinced that they weren't murderers. Take that vicar chap. When he was questioned by the police, just to get a picture, a feel of the place, he was always looking over his shoulder. Always checking to see who else was around. He was never a suspect but, his behaviour was strange. His everyday movements were erratic. He rode around the village, frantically weaving in and out of cars and pedestrians. His long neck seemed to be pushing his head out of his body. He greeted his parishioners along the way. He was a popular man. He always had the knack of fund-raising ideas for the church roof or organ. He had just persuaded an army of volunteers to paint the church hall, including the moody teenagers. What did he have to hide?

That bloke that worked in the graveyard and did odd jobs in the village was another strange one. He, almost, snarled when questioned about the murder. He was another one with no motive but, his reactions and attitude to the police were that of a guilty man, not guilty of murder, Alan Stock was sure of. What is his name? anyway, he was the complete opposite of the vicar, both in appearance and personality. He was short and stocky, unlike the gangly vicar. Just as the vicar was energetic, enthusiastic and lively, that chap was slow and never seemed to enjoy his work or, life.

That Landlord of the pub was another one with something to hide. Whenever I go into the pub his hand shakes when he pours the beer. Keith was a popular landlord. A bit grumpy. Not a jovial chap, more of a Basil Fawlty. He was married to Kath. Kath wouldn't say it was a happy marriage or, particularly un-happy, really. She was a cheerful, bubbly lady. She put up with Keith's moods as she liked the pub landlady life style. They didn't have any children so, the locals were her family. When she considered Keith's personality, she couldn't say that he was moody. No, his mood was always the same, miserable. Why had she married him? She was young, impressionable and thought that he was the best looking boy that she had ever seen. Her parents admired his honesty and work ethic. His lack of personality only seemed to bother Kath's friends, who could not understand why a lively girl would marry him. The locals liked Keith either, because of his straight forward honesty or, they enjoyed the "Fawlty Towers" experience. Kath was, as were the police, puzzled by Keith's recent behaviour. He was spending a lot of time with the vicar and that other chap, who looked after the church. Why the vicar? Keith didn't believe in God. Was he seeking forgiveness for his miserable ways? Kath doubted that was the reason. He enjoyed being miserable. She also noticed his fear of the police. She knew that he wasn't a murder suspect but, what was going on?

The worst gossips, in Alan Stock's opinion, were the women on the new estate. The old part of the village had gossips and busy bodies but, they all looked after each other. They were good hearted people with good intentions. He wasn't a man to judge people. Live and let live was his motto but, his opinion of the women on the posh estate that he had met, was not very high. He was glad his Jill wasn't like that. She moaned, to him, about her friends. Of course, she did but, it was never spiteful. Those estate women were always trying to outdo each other. In Alan's opinion most of them were spoilt brats. All except that Mrs Freeman. I do hope that she is not the murderer. I hope she sorts herself out with that young Watson. Hope she comes to her senses. She has a good family life.

Detective Chief Inspector Stock knew that James Watson, the young detective sergeant who had been assigned to work with him, had the makings of a good detective. He knew that one day he would achieve greatness. He may even be chief constable. James was dedicated and he worked hard. He knew that James had a goal in life. It was to be a good policeman. The DCI also knew that James's weakness was that he was having an affair with Caroline Freeman. They were both being blackmailed by Paul Robertson. Inspector Stock had taken James off the murder inquiry but, he was not going to report him for being involved with a possible suspect. He also suspected that James's eagerness to implicate Nick Freeman as the murderer was to clear the way for him to have a permanent relationship with Mrs Freeman. He would tell James that he knew everything and tell his superiors that James knew Mrs Freeman, therefore, making it impossible for James to work on the case. They hadn't seen the problem, at the start, and let him work with the DCI. What Alan's boss didn't know was that young Watson knew Mrs Freeman rather better than they thought. Of course, she was a suspect, as well. The problem would be solved without jeopardising James's future career.

DCI Stock discovered that Paul Robertson had been blackmailing James and Mrs Freeman whilst looking into Robertson's financial affairs. When Paul's room was searched a very large quantity of cash was found in the wardrobe. The DCI knew that a self-employed builder may take cash payments to avoid paying VAT and income tax but, he had previously found out that Mr. Robertson was a meticulous record keeper. Every job that he had carried out was invoiced correctly for labour and materials. Receipts and expenses were entered in a cash book. Income agreed with his bank statement and, on making enquiries he knew what work Paul had carried out. Where and when he worked. Frequent visits to the local pub were his only out of work activity, it seemed. He would not have had the time to do any cash in hand extras. Paul had no savings accounts. He had no aspirations to buy property or fast cars. He lived for today. Why was the cash hidden away? No large sums were withdrawn from his account. Apart from business transactions, only cash for everyday expenses, a pint or four were withdrawn. A regular payment to his landlady and his van expenses. The information that the police had gathered from locals is that Paul lived for today. They too, thought the pub seemed to be his only out of work activity. He wasn't a scruffy man out of work but, neither was he a fashion follower. No large amounts of cash were ever withdrawn from his account.

DCI Stock put two and two together when he realised that his Detective Sergeant and Mrs Freeman were being blackmailed by Paul Robertson. James and Caroline had both been withdrawing the same large amount of cash at regular intervals. When Paul's hidden cash was counted it equated to amounts withdrawn from Caroline's and James's account. After

Paul was murdered the withdrawals stopped. DCI Stock did not, for one second, think that his young sergeant was a murderer. His career was the most important aspect in his life. He also knew exactly where James was on the night of the murder. He was on a training course in London and this could be verified by several witnesses. The course tutor and the constable who James shared a room with, along with a few other delegates, were all drinking into the early hours of the morning with James. It would be impossible for him to have murdered Paul. Caroline Freeman was another matter.

Mrs Freeman was always nervous when the police called at her home. Of course, she was worried when her husband was arrested. She also discovered the body with her friend. She was bound to be agitated but, now the DCI knew she was being blackmailed, this changed the direction of the case.

"Mrs Freeman, can we have a word, Please?"

"Yes, of course. It's not about Nick again, is it? I thought that you had proved his innocence."

"No, it's not concerning your husband. We would like to ask you a few questions. We know that Mr. Robertson was blackmailing you and we think we know why but, perhaps you could explain. We will take a seat, if we may, Mrs Freeman?"

Caroline sat down, silently, in shock. This was the police. Of course, they would find out. She knew that James had been taken off the case. They were going to find out everything.

"Inspector, I didn't kill Paul."

"We never said you did. We just want you to tell us everything."

"I presume you know about James and I? We've known each other since we were children. He just came back into my life and, well please don't tell Nick. I love Nick and my girls. It's all finished, over now. Please?"

"Mrs Freeman, if you are innocent, and this has no bearing on Paul's murder, Nick doesn't need to know, from us but, it is a small village."

"Right, I'll make sure he doesn't find out. Paul was working on the house opposite. I'd never met him. Everyone was employing him to build extensions. We didn't need any work doing, so I had no reason to have anything to do with him. You know about the garage door and that's the first time I had encountered him for business but, he had visited before. One day he knocked at the door. I saw him walk across the road and thought he was going to ask if he could remove the man-hole cover. That happens a lot when anyone has work done near us," Caroline was nervously turning her engagement ring. "He just came straight out with it. He said he knew about me and James. He knew that James was a detective and, that I was married with children. He said that I could deliver the money weekly. He told me where he lived. He said that if he called on me, neighbours would be suspicious, especially Angela, who he knew would question me. I knew that there would be trouble if I didn't stick to the plan. I don't have use of the car, much. I had to bus into Newston. I had to make an excuse to Angela, to stop her driving me in. She always drove me anywhere that I needed to be. I told her that I was having regular dental treatment and would be a long time. I knew that she wouldn't want to hang about in Newston It's strange, though. Paul gave me the impression that he wasn't doing it for the money."

"Most people do blackmail for money. What makes you think that it wasn't for money?"

"Just women's intuition, I think. I don't think that Paul was materialistic. He just spends his money in the pub. That's what I hear."

"You even told your friend, Mrs Davies, that you didn't know Mr. Robertson."

"I know, I usually tell Angela everything but, this was just too much."

"Mrs Davies was aware of your relationship with Detective Constable Watson?"

"Yes," Caroline could feel her words shakily coming out of her mouth.

"We will have to take DNA samples from you. You can come to the station now and be back in time to pick up the girls."

DCI Stock knew that Caroline Freeman wasn't a killer. He just had to eliminate her.

"Yes, I'll get it over with. I didn't kill Paul."

"You know, I don't think for one minute that Mrs Freeman is our killer." DCI Stock confided in his new detective sergeant even before Caroline's DNA results had proved her innocence.

DCI Stock had seen Caroline's savings accounts statements when Nick Freeman had given him permission to go through the paperwork after he was arrested. He was surprised that Freeman hadn't questioned his wife's finances but, he probably trusted her and never looked at her bank statement. Anyway, he now had to prove that young James was also being blackmailed. James, he thought, was a careful lad as far as money was concerned. He had a few drinks with his colleagues. All of his social life seemed to revolve around his job. There didn't seem to be a woman in his life until, of course, he found out about Mrs Freeman. He owned his own flat, with a mortgage, in town. He enjoyed watching football and playing golf. He was married to the job. The DCI and James were having a drink one evening, whilst chatting to the locals in Barker's End. James asked if he could borrow money to buy his round. Just a temporary cash flow problem, boss, I'll pay you back. Alan Stock was not worried, at all, about the loan. What concerned him was that this was out of character.

"Everything all right, Lad? You haven't any money worries?"

"No, all ok. Just something has cropped up."

His boss wasn't convinced and his suspicious, detective mind was going to get to the bottom of this. James's mate, Mark, was having a leaving do. The pub was near the police station and the landlady was putting on a buffet. A bit of a spread they called it. James had prepared his speech. His mate was being promoted and moving away to join another force. The day before the leaving party James told his boss he wouldn't be able to make the do. He couldn't afford it. It then became quite a regular occurrence that James missed social gatherings. DCI Stock was now going to investigate.

The boss visited James one evening on the pretence that he had come to discuss the case. James was happy to let him into his flat. He would love to help out the boss but, why would he discuss it with him. He was no longer working on the case. The DCI had an idea. He offered to make coffee whilst James was taking a phone call from his Mum. Brilliant timing, thought the inspector. Mums want to know everything from if you're washing your socks to if you have a girlfriend. The boss chuckled to himself. The plan couldn't have worked out better. He would pour the contents of the milk carton down the sink. James had put the phone down and wandered into the kitchen.

"Out of milk, lad. Can't drink it black."

"That's ok. There is a corner shop. Opens until midnight. I won't be long."

Whilst James was out Alan Stock rummaged through the paperwork in James's drawer. My luck really is in, he thought to himself. A tidy murder victim and a tidy detective. He soon found the bank statements and large amount of cash were being withdrawn on regular intervals. The withdrawals had only recently started. In fact, the cash had started to disappear from the account the same time as Mrs Freeman had withdrawn cash. How could he get James to admit that he was being blackmailed?

"Good timing, I have just boiled the kettle. Thanks for nipping to the shop.

"That's ok, boss, I can't drink black coffee, either. I could have sworn I had milk, though."

James had never had a visit from his boss before. This wasn't about the case. He was sure of it. He knows about me and Caroline. I was so insistent that Nick was guilty. I'll have to be careful in future.

"Watson, lad. This is a bit delicate but, it's best I ask now. You know, informal, like. Do you have any connections with anyone in Barker's End? Someone who may be a suspect in our enquiries or, did you know the victim?"

"What do you mean? Is that why you're here?"

"Did you know Paul Robertson?"

James knew that he would have to tell the truth. If he didn't confess he knew he would be in trouble. He could lose his job. If he told him everything it would all work out. The inspector was a fair man. He would do all he could to save his job for him. He took him off to save any trouble.

"I'll start at the beginning."

"Good idea. I may need more coffee."

"Caroline Freeman and I grew up together. We were neighbours. Our parents were best friends. We spent all of our spare time together. Both of our families assumed that we would marry and everyone would live happily ever after. Caroline went to university and met Nick. To be honest, guv, I wasn't that bothered. It was both sets of parents who were upset. Nick was a good catch and we all just accepted the situation. I was doing well at police college and our lives changed. One day, I met Caroline, again, and she invited me to visit her house, for coffee. She'd got the girls by then and we were old friends. No harm in chatting about the olden days over coffee. You won't believe this but, when I got to her house she almost dragged me upstairs. Talk about bored housewife. She ripped off my shirt and trousers, well almost. She told me that sex with me had always been great. Anyway, I made frequent visits when I knew that Nick was away. Wouldn't you, Boss? It was handed to me, on a plate. The thing is, I started to have feelings for her, again. You know, like when we were young. I wanted us to be together. I would take care of the girls. I knew that it was wrong but, when I had chance to put Nick in the frame for murder, I took it. Please, you have taken me off the case. Keep it just between us. I didn't kill Robertson, honest."

"I know that you didn't kill Robertson. Your memory is not particularly good for a Detective, lad. You were in London on a course."

"My God, how could I have forgotten, at such a crucial time."

"I do know that Robertson was blackmailing you about your affair."

"Yes, he was. How do you know?"

"Ah, I'm a detective. He was blackmailing you and Mrs Freeman. Correct?"

"Yes, he knows, knew, everything, that bloke. Said nothing. We knew nothing about him but, he knew everything about everybody. I was just moving off from Caroline's drive, one day, when he stopped the car. He asked if he could get in. I couldn't understand what he would want with me and, then he told me his plan. I went along with it for Caroline's sake. I loved her and wanted to be with her but, if Nick found out she would never see me again. I was biding my time. Caroline told me that she had just made her first payment to Paul. She, like me though, didn't think that he was doing it for the money."

"Mrs Freeman did tell me that herself. I wonder what he was up too. As you are off the case, I'll think of something to tell them. Leave it to me. Shame, I enjoyed working with you. I would advise you to stay away from Mrs Freeman."

"It's over between us. The strain of the murder, Nick's arrest and just finding the body have caused her too much stress. She doesn't want excitement in her life." James gave a grin, also relieved that his boss would keep him out of trouble.

"Did her friend, Angela Davies, know about you two?"

"Yes. Caroline told her everything. Not about the blackmail. She told me that she didn't even want Angela in on that."

Alan Stock couldn't make out why the victim was blackmailing anyone. What was he going to do with the money?

This is a different one, thought Inspector Stock, as he drank his second cup of tea of the day. I know a few suspects with motives but, which one did it? Who murdered Paul Robertson?

"I'm not going in, today, Jill," he yelled out to his wife as she was loading the dish washer. "They can do without me for one day. I'm going to sit quietly in the study and solve this case, once and for all." You can supply me with tea, all day. That'll keep me thinking," he chuckled as he spoke.

"That's what you think, Alan Stock. I'm meeting Helen for coffee and lunch so, won't be back until 4pm, at the earliest."

"Well, I'll get my own tea and lunch. At least I will have the house to myself. With no vacuum cleaner whirring around in the background, I will be able to think."

Alan Stock was a contented man. His career hadn't helped family life but, Jill had raised his two sons, who had grown into decent young men who, thankfully, did not join the police force. Alan knew that he should have seen his family more but, he did enjoy his job. This case was just difficult to solve. Let's just put down the facts, on paper and get to the bottom of it, he thought to himself.

Paul Robertson wasn't popular but, he was very good at his job. He could have been having affairs with local women but, it was a lot of women so, a lot of husbands could be suspects. He was blackmailing Mrs Freeman and young Watson because he knew of their affair. Why did he hide the money in his wardrobe? Why didn't he spend it? Why was he really killed? The answer lies in the village.

Has this got anything to do with the murder that took place twenty five years ago? Highly unlikely. A serial killer who operates decades apart. Unless, of course, he has moved, and murders in other parts of the country could be linked. I'll have to get someone onto this, tomorrow. I'm pretty sure that young mother's death wasn't suicide. That is connected to Robertson's death. I'm sure of it.

That Watson is a stupid young fool. It's lucky that he has a strong alibi for the night of the murder. Getting himself mixed up with Mrs Freeman is a daft thing to do. I suppose we were all young, once. Alan Stock spent most of the day talking to himself. It helped him straighten things out, along with the tea. He thought a lot of James Watson. He treated him like a son and he knew he would make a good detective. He would just have to sort out his love life. Robertson was blackmailing Watson and Mrs Freeman. Caroline Freeman has a lot to lose. She's got those kiddies and her husbands a decent chap.

Caroline Freeman can be first on my list:

She has a strong motive. Paul Robertson was blackmailing her. She had her own savings but, sooner or later her money was going to run out. Her husband was bound to ask questions as I am sure that she didn't keep a lot of secrets from him. Well of course young Watson was the biggest secret but, not sure if she is the type of woman who can lead a double life for long. She's an intelligent woman. She would know that blackmailers don't stop at one payment. Mrs Freeman certainly had good reason to want Paul Robertson dead. Even if she had ended her affair, as James had told him, she couldn't risk her husband finding out about it. Her marriage would be over. Nick would probably apply for custody of the girls. She didn't have a job or any other means to support herself. Her life would be in ruins. Robertson's death would solve her problems. The question is, if she did kill him, how did she move the body? It had already been established that Robertson wasn't murdered where he was found. The Freemans had only one car. That had been examined when Nick Freeman was arrested. If Mrs. Freeman was the murderer she would have needed help. Who could have helped her and why?

Next on my list is Nick Freeman:

He has already been arrested, questioned and released. Mistakes could have been made He wouldn't be the first murderer to be released and then new evidence found to convict him. Young Watson had already confessed to wanting him out of the way. It could set him up for life with Caroline. He admitted all of this to me. He wanted to make Nick Freeman number one suspect. Let's just think for a minute that Freeman killed Robertson for another reason. This argument over the building work doesn't make sense. Freeman wouldn't kill him over that. We know that. We let him go. I consider myself quite a good judge of character. Nick Freeman hasn't got a temper. What if Freeman knew that Robertson was blackmailing his wife? He didn't know why. If he did it would be Watson or

Caroline that he would murder, surely. Could it be that he argued with Robertson over the blackmailing and during the argument he killed him, manslaughter? He never gave the impression that he knew about his wife's affair.

Chris Davies seems to be another one who had an argument with the victim over building work. At the start of this case arguments about Robertson's work dominated the investigation but, everyone you speak to agrees that Robertson was a good worker. Everyone who had work done was pleased with the result. These disagreements are nothing to do with his death. I am sure of that. Chris Davies is hardly ever in the village. Why would he want the local builder dead? He was seen having a discussion with him in a remote area. What was that about? Was Robertson having an affair with Mrs. Davies? I don't think that we have questioned her enough about that possibility. She's a very attractive, rich lady and her husband is away a lot. I must make a note to question her again.

There are still a couple of more suspects on my list. Mr. and Mrs Gilbert have a very good reason for wanting Robertson out of the way. We know that her husband's alibi, for the time of the murder, was that he was in bed with his wife but, now that she was seen out that evening, either one of them could be the killer. Robertson had destroyed Gilbert's career. He has undercut his quotations for carpentry work. John Gilbert has no income. He wife must work in the shop and take care of the children. The worry about their future must be hitting them hard. The same question: How would she move the body by herself or, were they in it together?

Hilary? She's that stuck up woman. Apparently, she's the only resident of Barkers End who never wanted Robertson to work on her house. I wonder why that is? Was there something going on between her and Robertson? What did we find when we investigated her past? That's the strange thing. We didn't find out anything about her. I think we need to do some more digging as far as Mrs Snooty is concerned. We know that Marcus, her husband, came from a wealthy family, who run a business. Have I forgotten him? Could he have killed Robertson because he found out that his wife was having an affair with the deceased? No, you don't want any more suspects but, you can find out about Mrs Snooty. That's the first task for tomorrow.

"Hello, Mrs Patterson. We would just like a quick word about Mr. Robertson, you know the builder chap, who was killed. I think that we have met before and this is Detective Sergeant Dunn."

"Yes, Chief Inspector Stock, I do know who you are and I do know that Mr. Robertson was murdered. What I don't know is how this has got anything to do with me."

"We are speaking to everyone who had any connection with Mr. Robertson. He was a very private person and we don't know much about him. I don't think that you wanted him to work on your house. Did you, Mrs. Patterson?"

"I don't know who told you that. There are a lot of gossips on this estate."

Yes, Mrs. Patterson but, most of them are your friends. Is that true, about you not wanting Mr Robertson to work here?"

"Well, yes, I suppose so. Look, the only reason that I told Marcus that I didn't want Paul to work here was that

I'd heard that he was rude and off hand. That kind of thing. I didn't want him upsetting the children if they were here. My son, especially, would be interested in his tools. You know, that sort of boy thing. Paul might get nasty with him if he asked too many questions. That's all."

"Yes, of course, Mrs. Patterson. That will be all for now."

"She's lying, Sir."

"Yes, I know that Sargent Dunn but, we will have to delve a bit more into Hilary."

What about Robertson's landlady? She had nothing but praise for him. Did she though, was there anything going on that we don't know about? No, forget that one Stock. You will end up with too many suspects.

The pub landlord, Keith what's- his- name? Why would he kill him? Paul was a good customer. Drank quite a lot but, never caused serious trouble. Was just a bit aggressive, a bit loud? This was out of character for him. Robertson was a noticeably quiet man. Kept himself to himself. Was this what everyone was afraid of? He didn't say a lot but, knew a lot. Were the locals afraid that their secrets would come out when he had been drinking?

There are so many people that we haven't questioned, the vicar. He's a strange chap but, that doesn't make him a murderer. That church hall caretaker acts very strange when we are around but, so do a lot of people. Guilty conscience. Teachers, shop keepers, all sorts of village people but, nobody really knew Paul Robertston. No, stick to the people with motives. This isn't Midsomer Murders, Stock. No strange tales are going to come out of the woodwork. Tomorrow re-question the main suspects.

"Hello, love. Did you have a good day?"

"Lovely, really enjoyed ourselves. Did you manage to solve the case?"

"No, not really but, I do have a plan of action," Alan Stock kissed his wife on the cheek as he left the study to make them both a cup of tea.

I mustn't forget, Alan was now talking loudly to himself, that young woman who died. We are not going to treat that as suicide. These two deaths must be connected. How? We can find nothing to link Viv and Paul. She didn't have any work done on her home. She didn't mix, much, with the estate women. I'm sure she wasn't having an affair with Robertson. How could she? The only person to look after her child, if she was seeing anyone, was that neighbour. She would know what was going on. That young Viv wouldn't risk her finding out any secrets. Could Robertson have murdered Viv? Then why would he have been killed, himself? Perhaps question that nosey neighbour again. Find out if the victims were connected.

"You know what, Dunn. I don't think that young woman committed suicide. I believe her husband, poor chap, and that gossipy neighbour."

"Really, Sir?"

"Yes, really. These deaths are connected. There is something going on in this village. The poor girl had no reason to kill herself. She had everything to live for. We can't find out anything about her to suggest problems in her life. Dunn, we interviewed her husband, her distraught parents, in-laws, old friends and work colleagues. Not one of them gave the impression that Viv had any worries, and certainly not suicidal."

"I know, Sir but, suicide victims often don't show any signs to anyone else. They really do keep it all to themselves. Just say, she wasn't sleeping. Her husband wouldn't know. He could be out, like a log, every night. I bet you don't know when your wife is awake. Believe me, she is a mother and my Mum told me that you don't sleep once you become a mother. That gossipy neighbour of hers says so much, she wouldn't notice if Viv was unhappy. Anyway, Viv would put on a brave face for her family and friends. I've just done on course on suicide, Sir. We can't find out anything about Paul Robertson, either and he was not popular.

"Course, or not, Dunn, I'm convinced that the two deaths are connected.

He had no known family, partner or friends. It's different for that Viv. Nice little family girl, by all accounts. We are going to treat her death as murder. In such a small place it must be linked to the other one. It may make our investigations easier."

"Right boss, what's next?"

"I will have to work that out, Dunn."

That young Mum didn't commit suicide, said Alan Stock, to himself. Yes, I admit that's what it looked like at first. That was before that Robertson chap got himself killed. There must be a connection. Two murders don't happen in a village. We must be looking for one killer. DCI Stock did question, Yvonne, again, and found out some interesting facts that did link the two deaths. What Viv had discovered about Paul Robertson made some sense. Did he kill Viv but, then who killed him?

Chapter 10

Chris Davies is a successful solicitor who runs his own business in Barker's End. He works from home but, spends most of his time visiting his clients. He married Angela when they were both in their twenties. He never meant to marry Angela. He was just about to propose to his girlfriend but, then there she was. Angela gave him her telephone number, to help him choose gifts for his fiancé, or, that's what he thought.

"I'd love to go out with you but, you already have a girlfriend. A fiancé, actually. I know that you do. That's how we met. You were buying her perfume from me," Angela whispered, coyly, into the telephone, in her parent's hallway. She knew exactly what she was doing. She knew that she could break up his relationship. He was the most attractive man that she had ever met, and she was going to lure him away.

Chris sat watching television, with his parents.

"It's not like you, to grace us with your presence, in an evening. Not seeing Jane, this evening?" His father spoke when there was a break for the advertisements. He left the room to telephone Angela.

"I don't know how to say this but, it's all over between me and Jane."

"What, I am sorry. You spent all that money on perfume. What went wrong?" Angela was a good liar. She faked sympathy, perfectly.

"Oh, nothing, really, a build-up, you know," Chris was lying as Angela was the reason for the break up.

Telling Angela was one thing. How was he going to break the news to his parents? The best thing, or so he thought, was just to bring Angela home. Dive straight in. Face the consequences.

"I am bringing someone to meet you, tomorrow evening. After dinner. We don't want to make a fuss and, we don't want you cooking for us, Mum."

The next evening came far too slowly for Chris's parents.

"Mum, Dad, this is Angela," Chris nervously introduced his new girlfriend to his parents, knowing what their reaction would be.

"Pleased to meet you, love," his father reached out to shake the attractive girl's hand.

"Tea or coffee, Angela? Chris, can you just pop into the kitchen and reach the cups for me?"

Chris, dutifully, followed his mother into the kitchen.

"Who's this? What happened to Jane? You were going to marry her. You told us. Lovely girl, she was, is. What's going on, Chris? What happened? You were so right for each other. I don't know what's got into you. Just because you are brainy enough to be a fancy solicitor. You had known her ages. When you said you were getting engaged I even bought a suit." Chris's mother was near to tears as she poured the tea.

"Too many questions for me to answer at once, Mum. Jane and I, well. We just drifted apart."

"Drifted apart. You mean that fancy piece in there turned your head. I don't know what your father will have to say about this. Jane was like a daughter to us."

Chris and Angela spent every spare minute together.

"Angela and I are going to be married. You will grow to love Angela, if you give her a chance."

Chris's parents couldn't understand why he would want to marry Angela instead of Jane.

"She's one of us, is Jane. Such a lovely little thing. I was really looking forward to having girlie outings with Jane. Can't see me getting on with Angela."

"Look, Mum, I am marrying Angela, you're not. It's my life and my happiness we're talking about," Chris slammed his fist on the table, as he shouted at his mother.

"Now, son. Don't shout at your mother. Have some respect. She's got a point, you know. That girl is very attractive but, she may not make you happy."

"Dad, you said yourself that you married the most beautiful woman that you had ever seen. Didn't she make you happy? Isn't she a good wife and mother?"

"You're right there, son. Me and your Mum are just a bit shocked, that's all. It's your life and for your sake, we hope that this all works out."

"It will, Dad. Don't you two worry. It will all be fine."

Chris's Mum then went into the kitchen to do the only thing that helps in a crisis. She made a cup of tea.

"Oh, Chris, they don't like me."

"It's not that. They don't know you, like I do. It's just that me and Jane had been together for a long time. They knew her well, that's all. You just wait until they get to know you. They will love you like I do. It's just a shock. You know, us getting married. I just know that you are the one. We will be together forever." He lifted her up into his arms and swung her around.

"Oh Chris. I am so happy. I will do anything for you."

Chris's parents never approved of Angela. She wasn't down to earth, like Jane. They reluctantly came to the wedding but, didn't visit Chris and Angela when they moved to Barker's End. Chris did go to see them, occasionally, on his own but, the visits were formal and strained.

Chris never regretted marrying the most beautiful woman that he had ever seen. They were meant to be together. Angela was not only good to look at. She organised him, was charming to his dinner guests and, they loved each other. The locals regard them as the celebrity couple. She loved the village life. She is never happier than when organising the fete, the coffee mornings. You name it, Angela organised it. She had friends in the village. Chris wasn't bothered about village life but, he did enjoy the pub chat, especially with Nick Freeman. Life couldn't be any better for Chris. The village is a pleasant place to live for Chris. When he is there he is at his wife's side.

For many of the women in the village Angela's attraction was that, despite not having children, she did not go out to work. Most of the women had children and a career. They spent their lives permanently stressed whilst Angela swanned around in her finery every day. What Angela's friends didn't know is that Chris was always having affairs. Angela turned a blind eye to Chris's behaviour. She didn't want to give up her lifestyle and, she did love him. Chris met women when he stayed away, in hotels. He missed Angela. He loved Angela.

Chris had forgotten his flings when he checked out the next day. It was just a distraction. The women felt the same. They were, too, looking for entertainment away from home. This was just going to be the latest.

"Hello, I'm Chris," he said cheerily before offering to buy the lady, sitting at the bar, a drink.

"Oh, nice to meet you, I'm Karen."

One thing led to another and they ended up in Chris's room.

"Oh, sorry to wake you but, I have to be at a meeting, very soon." What did he see in this one, he thought to himself. I will really have to stop doing this. Why doesn't he buy a book, play games on his laptop? Why does he go to bed with these women, who he doesn't even fancy? He has Angela. He never used to be like this. He must have that disease where you go and see a counsellor because you need sex.

Another trip and another woman at the bar.

"Good evening, do you come here often?"

"No, first and probably the last time. Do you really use that chat up line on men?"

"Not all of the time," laughed Eve. "I'm Eve and you are?"

"Chris. I'm just here for one night. I had a meeting in the town. Back home tomorrow."

"Lovely to meet you, Chris. What was your meeting about? What do you do?"

"I'm a solicitor. Clients all over the place so, I'm away from home a lot."

A Solicitor, really. We will get on well. I'm just here to set up a new office for my boss. I'm not exactly a solicitor, not clever, like you. I'm an office manager for a law firm. I am here recruiting staff for a new branch."

"I must buy you a drink. We must have so much in common. What would you like?"

"Just a white wine, please. Very dry."

Eve and Chris chatted for most of the evening. They had the law in common. Chris found Eve more interesting than most of his one-night-stands. Eve was married and, like him, didn't have children to get in the way of her career, as she put it.

The inevitable happened and they spent the night in her room. This wasn't unusual for Chris but, what was unusual was that he enjoyed her company. He didn't want to leave her in the morning. No, he said to himself. This didn't happen. He was going home to the love of his life. He would put Eve out of his mind. He wasn't falling in love with her after one fling.

Chris may have decided to put Eve out of his mind but, Eve had other ideas. She was not married to the love of her life. Hers was not a happy marriage. She had really fallen for Chris. Life for Chris carried on as normal.

"Chris, whilst you were out you had a call. A lady called Eve. She didn't give her surname or details of the case. I just took her number." Sue was efficient. Chris thanked her. He was puzzled He didn't give Eve his number. He never gave them his office number. He did have another mobile which he sometimes used for his other life. That was really if they were going to be in the same place again. This rarely happened. How did she get this number? He wasn't that drunk. He wasn't drunk at all. Only some of his clients knew this number. He did most of his work at home. This was just a registered office.

Sue was only part-time. That's all he needed. He had offered Angela the job but, she wasn't going to work. She had everybody else to organise.

"Chris, I didn't know what to tell her. That woman, Eve, called again. She must need a solicitor desperately."

Chris admired Sue's tact.

"I'll phone her back. She did leave her number?"

Sue left the room, quietly closing the door.

"Eve, how did you get this number?"

"Chris, I work with solicitors. People who delve," she giggled into the phone. "It was easy to find you. You don't answer my calls."

"Eve, you know that we were not going to meet again. You were not my first one night stand and you are not going to be my last."

Chris knew that he was being hurtful and, he didn't want to hurt Eve. He called her back. He did want to see her again. He met Eve on several occasions at various locations. They always met at hotels where no one would know them. They chatted over bottles of wine and Chris felt very relaxed. He couldn't help falling for her. Eve wasn't like the others. Eve and Chris even started spending days together without sex. They enjoyed trips to the theatre. Was this the one. Would he leave Angela for her? He was going to have to put a stop to this. He now had another distraction in his life, with a visit from the police.

"Good afternoon Mrs Davies," DCI Stock showed his warrant card as he entered the hallway.

"Oh, Hello, would you like tea or coffee?" asked Angela as she led the detective into the living room. "Do you want to ask me some questions about Paul? You know that I am happy to help, if I can."

"No, it's Mr. Davies that we have come to see."

"Really?" replied Angela, nervously. "He's in the study. Chris, the police are here to see you." Angela tried to sound unperturbed but, she couldn't hide the panic in her voice. Why would the police want to question him?"

"Good afternoon, Mr. Davies. We just need to clear up a few points regarding your original statement. When we last spoke to you we established that you were away when Mr. Robertson was murdered."

"Yes, that's right. You have all my appointments in the diary. Don't you Angela?"

"Yes, but, we told you this Inspector, at the very start of all this."

"Yes, I know, Mrs Davies, and we have confirmed with a Mr. Rogers that your husband was in Cambridge when the murder was committed but, a witness has come forward to say that Mr. Davies was seen talking to Mr. Robertson about a week before he was murdered."

"I am here, Angela. I can speak for myself. You haven't got that tea, yet, for the Inspector."

"He didn't want any. Did you?" Angela tried not to show her emotions.

"I never say no to tea, Mrs Davies, three sugars, if you remember."

The cups on the tray were wobbling as Angela entered the room. Her calm and cool demeanour had left her.

"I'll take the tray, Mrs Davies, thank you."

Chris was now pacing the floor.

"What date was I seen? I will have to look in the diary. Angela, love, please go and fetch the diary. Ah, that's it. I was in Cambridge, then. I had to make two visits."

"Thank you for clearing that up, Sir. I'll carry on, shall I? The witness recognised your car. It was just outside the village. They were walking their dog and were surprised to see the driver of the vehicle having a heated, as they put it, discussion with Paul. Of course, Mr. Davies, someone else may have been driving your car that evening. Is that the case? If so, then may we have the name of the driver, please? The witness is sure that the other man in the car was Mr. Robertson. They had seen him leaving the pub, earlier. A strange time and place for a discussion?"

"I'm not going to lie. It was me in the car. It was Paul Robertson I was arguing with. I left my meeting earlier than expected and, instead of staying overnight, I came back to see Robertson. You see, I wanted to question him about the bill he had sent to us for the work he carried out in the house."

"Chris, why didn't I know about this? You never came here for the night. What's all this about? Angela was anxious. This wasn't her husband's usual behaviour, even when he was seeing other women.

"You weren't expecting me back. I didn't want to frighten you. If you woke up and heard me coming into the house, you may have thought it was burglars. I know you, Angela. You may have wacked me over the head with a saucepan or, worse, got out a kitchen knife." Chris's attempt to lighten the mood failed to impress Angela or the DCI.

"I met Paul, in secret, to protect you. If I had met him in the pub, the usual gossips would have, no doubt, informed you of our disagreement. You would have been upset about the bill and I just wanted to sort everything out without you knowing."

"Yes, Mr. Davies. That sounds a good reason for the meeting. Thanks for clearing that up. I'll see myself out."

Chris was telling the truth about his accommodation that night.

"I can't make head or tail of any of this. Can you? If you look at the evidence we have, this murder is all about building work but, I don't think that Robertson's quality of work or, fees have anything to do with his death. Could he have been blackmailing someone else in this village? That's my bet. I think that we have been looking at this from the wrong angle. I don't believe a word that Chris Davies said. Would you really meet someone that late at night, in a remote location about a disagreement with a bill? We'll go along with this for now. We don't have evidence but, I am not letting Davies off the hook."

"Boss. I still think that Nick Freeman is the main suspect. I know that the rope didn't match and there is no real evidence but, I think that if we keep digging, we can find some more evidence to convict him."

"I think that you have been talking to Watson. Nick Freeman has nothing to do with this," replied, a rather irritated, Alan Stock.

Angela spoke calmly, at first, to her husband, after the police had left them.

"The police may have been satisfied with that rubbish coming out of your mouth but, I'm not. This is me, Angela, your wife." Angela slammed her mug on the worktop.

"It's the truth. What else can I say."

"This is what I think. You are up to your old tricks again. Who is she this time? Had Paul seen you with her and you were paying him to keep quiet? Where did you stay that night?

"Just a B and B in the village."

"Give me the name, telephone number."

"OK, phone them."

"I will phone them, don't you worry. Remember, I know everyone in this village. Viv is friends with the woman, Marge, is her name. She runs the B and B."

"I won't discuss this with you, anymore, Angela, I've told you the truth."

Angela would get to the bottom of this. She was determined.

Chris was surprised that the police called him on his mobile, soon after they had left the house.

"Mr. Davies?"

"Yes."

"It's DCI Stock. We thought that you would like to come to the police station. Have a chat, out of the way of Mrs. Davies. You may be able to tell us the real reason that you met Mr. Roberston that night. You know, away from your wife."

"Yes, I'll be there soon."

"When you're ready, Mr. Davies. Was Robertson blackmailing you or, was he having an affair with your wife?"

"No, what makes you say that?"

It's just that you wouldn't be the first resident of Barker's End to be blackmailed by him. Were you having an affair that he found out about? You see, Mr. Davies, nobody believes your story about meeting him about a job. In fact, I'm sure Mrs Davies doesn't believe a word of it."

"You're right there. Angela doesn't believe me. Right, the truth but, I'd rather Angela didn't know. Not now he is dead. Not now it's all over."

"What's all over, Mr Davies?"

"Paul Robertson and I were going to run away together. We had been seeing each other."

Alan Stock was a man of the world. He had to be in his job. He had seen everything. He was still old fashioned and, in his world men still ran off with women. This wasn't London. He didn't see this twist in the tale.

"It's hard to believe, myself. I had always been happy with Angela. I'd had one night stands with other woman but, a man, no way. That's what I thought.

I'd gone to the pub one evening. I usually only go with Nick Freeman. The other blokes are fine but, Nick and I are real mates. Although he had no idea about me and Paul. Nobody did. Nick and I met through our wives but, Nick's a good bloke. Anyway, he was away. I had an unusually free evening. I'm away or, entertaining most evenings. Angela was at one of her women's things. I just fancied a pint. The pub was busy for a week-day evening. There was one seat left, up in the corner. Paul was sitting there by himself, as usual. I asked him if I could join him. He just mumbled. I only knew him through his building work. Strange bloke, never spoke to anyone. Didn't say much when he was working. That's a good thing, I suppose. He just got on with it. Did a good job. We got chatting, surprisingly enough. We had too, really. That table was a bit cramped. We stayed until closing time. He was interesting. He never talked about himself or, his private life. He discussed a lot of topics. Current affairs, you know. He had never said much before but, he seemed to know everything. We said our goodbyes and I asked him if we could meet again for another chat and pint. I said that we would meet outside of the village. I don't know why I said that.

We met a few times at various pubs. We were both driving so didn't drink but, we often had meals out. Angela just thought that I was with clients. The more that I met him the more that I couldn't stop thinking about him. It was a strange feeling. Nick was a mate but, Paul, meant something to me. I didn't know what was going on. I couldn't turn to anyone. Perhaps I was his only friend and he was glad to meet me. I wanted to find out if he felt the same way as me. I was being daft. He was a ladies man. So was I.

When we were planning our next outing I told him that I would pick him up from his digs in Newston. I just wanted to gauge the situation. I wanted to know about his relationships with women. I needed to know how ridiculous I was acting. I wasn't just going to tell another bloke that I loved him. I picked Paul up. He always left his van at his digs when he came back to the village pub. He had a taxi there and back. I asked him why he bothered with this as there were pubs in Newston. He said they were all gastro-pubs and posh food. He told me that it was all lies about his affairs with women on the estate. He wanted to keep people guessing. It was his little game. He told me that he went out with Angela, as a friend. I knew that they had been seen together. He told me something about his past. I asked him, outright, if he had ever considered a gay affair. I expected him to lose his temper, leave the car, slam the door, walk home. He didn't. He told me that he had grown to love me. He said it was daft. I was married to Angela, for god's sake. She is the most attractive, vivacious woman you could ever meet. As you have probably found out, I did have one night stands with other women but, they meant nothing.

I loved, love Angela. Paul was the complete opposite of Angela. He was quiet and introverted. I couldn't believe what was happening to me. I confessed my feelings towards him. He got another mobile phone, just so that we could arrange meetings.

That was the start, really. We carried on seeing each other. We planned, carefully, that we were going to be together. His life would carry on the same. My life was going to change, completely. I didn't care, this is who I wanted to be with forever.

That night, Inspector, when we were seen in the car, we were arguing about our plans. We both had loose ends to tie up. We just couldn't agree on the timing.

I didn't kill him, Inspector. I wouldn't. I loved him. He loved me. I was really away on the night that he was murdered."

"I know you were, Mr. Davies. We have already checked. So, tell us, when did Mrs. Davies find out about your relationship?"

"She became suspicious when you came round, about our late night meeting."

"Yes, why were you and Robertson in the car when, I'm sure, you could afford more comfortable surroundings, hotel rooms?"

"It was just that Paul had a lot of work on. He was working all hours. He was very conscientious. He wouldn't leave the area until he had finished every last job. We were finalising our getaway."

"The witness said that you had a heated argument."

"Only because we couldn't agree on a date to leave."

"And, Mrs Davies."

194

"Angela started to delve and got her village spies to check up on us, I think but, I have an idea that she found out from Paul."

"There is another suspicious death in the village. You are probably aware that a young mother died."

"Yes, Viv, I think her name is, was. What's that got to do with me and Paul? Angela told me that she had committed suicide. I don't know anything about her. She did come to the house, I think. Angela had a lot of friends in the village. I don't know them all."

"You see, Mr. Davies, this is a village. You must realise, yourself, that two suspicious deaths in one village are unusual. This isn't the Bronx."

"Yes, I see what you mean but, I just thought that her death was suicide. I never connected them."

"Thank you, Mr. Davies, you are free to go."

For the first time during this enquiry, Alan Stock knew that he was getting somewhere.

Chapter 11

"Hello, Mrs Davies. May we come in, please?"

"Yes, I am seeing rather a lot of you, lately."

"Angela Davies, I am arresting you for the murder of Paul Robertson. You don't have to say anything."

"I know all that. Let's get this over with. Take me to the police station. I'll be home soon. I didn't do it and presume I can ring my solicitor when I get there."

"I must say that you are very calm about this, Mrs Davies."

"Inspector Stock, sorry Detective Chief Inspector Stock, I told you I am not guilty so, nothing to be worried about."

Angela walked calmly to the police car, waiting outside. She was aware that her neighbour was watching.

"We have now switched on the tape, Mrs Davies. When police officers visited your house, we, told you that we had information that you spent time with Mr. Robertson. You did meet him for lunch on several occasions? Is that true, Mrs Davies?"

"Yes, that is correct. We did meet for lunch a few times. The rest of the village were rather hostile towards Paul, Mr. Robertson. The men and women seem to think that he was unfriendly and rather uncouth. When he was with me, I saw a different side to him. He was interesting to talk to. He was quiet and thoughtful. I enjoyed his company."

"Were you and Mr. Robertson having an affair?"

"No, we were just friends, that's the truth," replied Angela, without hesitation.

"You see, Mrs Davies, we looked through Mr. Robertson's bank account and receipts. He purchased a few items of jewellery and we could find no evidence that there was a woman in his life. Not even a mother or sister."

"Yes, Paul did buy me some gifts. I'm not sure myself why he did it. Perhaps, like me, he valued our friendship. It could have been his way of thanking me for being his only friend or, putting a lot of work his way."

"I think that you were incensed that Mr Robertson didn't want to start a relationship with you. Most men found you extremely attractive. This was damaging enough for your ego but, the real shock and hurt was that Paul Robertson was planning to start a new life with your husband. This would be devastating for most women but, for someone like you, with the perfect marriage and perfect looks this was too much to bear. The shame it would bring. Your life, as you knew it, had ended."

"You, and your friends, had spent a lot of time trying to find out about Mr Robertson's personal relationships. We believe, Mrs Davies, that it was you who, perhaps, by chance found the answer to the question you had all been asking. You couldn't believe it, could you Mrs. Davies? Your husband, Chris, had been having affairs, or, one-night-stands for ages. You accepted this. The other women never meant anything to him. He loved you. You made a great team. You had money. Your friends, in the village, looked up to you. You enjoyed the committee work. Life was perfect. You found out that his latest affair wasn't a fling to pass the time. Chris was leaving you. To make matters worse, he was leaving you for another man. A man that you had tried to entice into bed. A man who you thought was having affairs with your friends."

"I just couldn't take it. The leaving me. The humiliation. I could cope without Chris but, the shame. I would have to leave the village." Angela was sobbing into her hands.

"You see, at first, Mrs Davies, we didn't think that a woman would have the strength to move the body. We went back to investigate the murder scene. This is when we realised that we had missed something. A vehicle could get through the clearing in the woods. Close to where the body was found."

"I didn't kill him but, I wanted to make him see sense. He had already told me about his plans to run away with Chris. I am surprised that he agreed to see me that evening. He probably felt sorry for me. He didn't need Chris. I did. He was used to being alone. All he had to do was leave the area. He'd moved around before. He could find work, anywhere. I offered him money. He wouldn't take it. You see, I met him in the pub, that evening. I knew that the men were away. A cricket match. Chris was away, as well. The pub landlord, Keith, wasn't working that evening. The girl behind the bar didn't know me. That bit I had planned. I didn't want the gossip spreading around the village that I was seen with Paul. I bought Paul a few drinks. He then relaxed. After all, it wasn't an ideal situation, to be in drinking with your lover's wife. He was happy for us to be the only customers in the pub, that evening. He always got a taxi to and from Newston to the village pub in the evening. I had asked him why he didn't drink in Newston, especially, when he didn't speak to the locals, anyway. He said that the pubs in Newston were those posh Gastro places. No good for a quiet pint."

"Carry on, Mrs Davies."

"I offered to drive him back. I told him not to call a taxi. He thought that I was drinking gin and tonic but, I only had tonic, so I could drive. He was nearly asleep when we left the pub. He wasn't used to the shorts that I had been plying him with. That's all, really. I just drove him back to his digs and he got out of the car. That's it."

"No, Mrs Davies, we don't think that is it. It's not what happened, is it? You see, his landlady got up in the night and she knew that he wasn't at home. She worries about him, like she would a son. He always told her when he wasn't coming home. Which, incidentally, was on quite a few occasions, probably since he had met your husband. You didn't drive Mr. Roberston home, did you?"

After a lot of denying and sobbing, Angela couldn't lie anymore.

"No, alright. The rope was in the glove compartment. I hadn't planned it, really. I'd taken the rope from Caroline and Nick's garage. I was going to use it on our back gate until Chris brought a new catch. Chris wasn't going to pay anyone to do that simple job. I had never planned to kill Paul. He was asleep so I had more time to think about the situation. I was getting angry. I pulled into the lane that led to the woods and just did it. I pulled the rope tightly around his neck. Of course, he woke up, tried to struggle but, I'm stronger than I look.

I must have just got lucky, I suppose. I didn't even know that he was dead. I had to drive the car further into the woods, tip Paul out and drag him to. Look, you know the rest."

"Why did you let Mrs Freeman find the body when she was with you? It may not have been found for weeks."

"When I got home I realised that Caroline wouldn't remember me asking for the rope. She knows that I am not the sort of woman that rummages around in a garage. I had the idea of framing Nick for the murder."

"Mrs Freeman is your best friend."

"She is but, you always have to put yourself first. She'd be ok. If Nick went to prison she would have your sergeant to take care of her."

"Mrs Davies, although we are having a hard job finding evidence, we now think that you are responsible for an earlier murder in Barker's End."

I can't believe that you just said that. I did hear something about a farmer's wife being murdered years ago but, I was hardly born."

"No, not that Mrs Davies. A young woman with a child. A lady, who I believe, was a friend of yours. You see, Mrs Davies, we know that you have a lot of friends and, one of them is a very talkative lady. Bye the way, do you pass old magazines onto your friends?"

"It's no crime to be popular and whatever has magazines got to do with this? No I take them to the library. It saves them having to buy them. They are always in good condition are still up to date when I have finished with them."

"You won't have passed them on to anyone but the library, then?"

"No, why are you asking?"

"Well, you probably know who the talkative friend is."

"I could guess."

"Yvonne is a very helpful lady."

"I bet she is."

"Yvonne has told us that she read a story in a magazine. It was about someone being poisoned by cherry stones."

"What has that got to do with me?"

"Who's been murdered by cherry pips? A likely story. That's what it is a story."

"One of your friends, Mrs Davies. A very young woman, with a child. That's who has been murdered this way."

"She was depressed. She killed herself. She was lonely. Stuck with a child, all day."

"We don't believe that to be the case. She wasn't lonely or, depressed. We believe but, of course, we have to prove it, that you killed her." We know that you made her a cake, using fresh cherries. Your talkative friend told us that. We believe that you put ground-up cherry stones into the cake that you made her. Cherry stones, when ground up, turn to cyanide in the body."

"How would I know that? I've never been any good at science. She was a scientist, you know. Viv, that's how she knew how to kill herself."

"The story in the magazine is about a murder being committed in this way. You would know this, Mrs Davies, after reading the magazine, that you passed on."

"I have never read anything like that. Well, what's my motive?"

"There again, Mrs Davies, Yvonne is very helpful. Viv was getting very close to finding out who Mr. Robertson was in a relationship with. You had already guessed that it was your husband. You would not want the scandal to spread around the village. You know that Yvonne would be an expert at rumour spreading but, she didn't know, did she? Viv would be easier to dispose of. You may not have meant to kill Paul Robertson but, you planned the murder of a young woman."

The cell door closed. Angela knew that she had to accept her fate.

Caroline had no idea where her friend was.

"Hello, is Angela away Mrs Allan? It's funny she didn't tell me."

"No dear. I suppose you don't know. The police came yesterday and she went off with them. I wouldn't usually notice these things but, I was cleaning the front window. I keep myself to myself. I don't think that she came back."

"What do you mean, she didn't come back?"

Caroline got home and picked up the phone. "James, you must tell me what's going on. Why have they taken Angela? Is it anything to do with Paul?"

"You know that I can't tell you. I will let you know as soon as I can," and James hung up.

Caroline stayed at home all day. She couldn't contact Nick. He must be on the motorway. She didn't have anyone else to talk to. She couldn't go to the police station. They wouldn't tell her what was happening. Later she would go back and talk to Jean Allen, Angela's neighbour. Chris might be home. Angela might be home. They wouldn't be keeping her long. She hasn't done anything wrong. Caroline had asked her neighbour to come in and look after the girls. They had gone to bed. They wouldn't know that she was out. She didn't tell her daughters about Angela. There wouldn't be anything to tell, would there?

"Hello Jean, Mrs Allen. Is Angela back? I can't make her hear. Where's Chris?"

"He is there, dear. I think so, as his car is in the garage."

"I'll speak to him, then. Thank you, Mrs. Allen."

"Chris, are you in there? Let me in. It's Caroline. I can see you through the window. What's wrong? Let me in."

Chris didn't answer the door to Caroline. She went home wondering what to do next. The police wouldn't tell her anything. She would ask Nick to come home.

"Nick, please, are you on your way home?"

"Yes, what's wrong? It's not the police visiting us, again, is it? Are the girls ok?"

"Everything with us is fine. I will tell you when you get home. Please hurry."

After Angela's trial Caroline tried to contact Chris again. She hadn't seen him since Angela's arrest. She couldn't believe that her friend was a murderer but, Angela was convicted and sent to prison. She doesn't want any visitors, including her husband or, her best friend.

"Chris, I know that you are in there. I'm your friend. Nobody's seen you for months. Nick and I will support you. Have you been to see her?"

Chris eventually opens the door to Caroline.

"Oh, your case. Are you going away on a business trip?"

"No, Caroline. I would have gone sooner but, I had loose ends to tie up, with work. I'm leaving for good. Too many bad memories. I'm selling the house. Angela doesn't want to see me. She may come round. Who knows. You won't believe this but, I will always love her. I can't face the gossip, here. I was never part of the village as you and Angela were."

"Nick and I will help you get through this. We don't judge."

"No. Caroline. I've lost Angela and Paul. I loved them both. Paul just seemed to be what I had always wanted in a partner. Bye, Caroline."

For the second time in two days, Caroline ran home. This time she was crying.

"Thank you, Mrs Mason, for staying with the girls."

"Is everything all right? Do you want me to stay?"

"No, Nick will be home soon," she lied.

Caroline opened the fridge door and filled a large glass with wine. She did wonder why she bothered with the glass. Why not drink straight from the bottle. When she woke up the sun was streaming through the curtains.

"Mummy, you haven't been to bed. Why are you sleeping down here? You are not ill, are you? Should we fetch Angela?"

"No, I'm fine. Just fell asleep watching a programme I like. I must have been tired. Angela has gone away for a little holiday, anyway. I will just shower and then we will have some breakfast."

At the school gate Caroline had to answer the endless questions about Angela, Chris and Paul, even though it was now on the front page of the local paper. The truth was there for all to see. Or at least the media's version of the truth. She didn't know any more than anyone else.

Of Course, rumours had started and speculations voiced, with everyone having an opinion of how this all could have happened. Nick would be back this afternoon. At least she would have a friend.

The days went by and Nick took a few days off work to spend with Caroline. Nick went back to work but, Caroline was still not coping with her friend's imprisonment. The phone rang one morning as Caroline was making the beds. She spent her days cleaning and drinking.

"Hello James."

"I'll pop round. See you soon."

"James, I'm so glad to see you. I can't believe what has happened."

"Let me get through the door. Nick away?"

"He will be back later. He is in the local office. He doesn't want to leave me to long on my own."

"I'll Just tell you everything, now that the trial is over."

Angela was desperate to have an affair with Paul. I think that he was the only man not to be attracted to her. Of Course, we now know that there was a good reason for that. He was having an affair with Chris. Paul, in spite of what the gossip led us to believe, had never had an affair with a woman. Angela discovered the night before she killed Paul that he was running away with Chris.

There was evidence that Angela's car was parked in the lane near where Paul's body was found."

"What lane? I have walked that route many times, with Angela, and there isn't a lane."

"There is but, you have to know where it leads to. You have to go into a wooded area, near the footpath.

You can just about get a car into the lane. It's hardly used. Angela, obviously knew where it was. She could have dragged the body by herself It wasn't too far. Chris was away, nobody knew that she was missing."

"Well, I presumed she killed Paul because he was running away with her husband. A pretty good motive, if you ask me," Caroline was still shocked by the whole situation.

"Obviously, that is enough for a motive but, her ego was also bruised. All men fancied Angela but, this one man was more interested in her husband. She was even jealous that you and me were having an affair."

"What, why?"

"Oh, I won't flatter myself. She didn't fancy me. It was the thought of her mousey, goody, little friend having a bit of excitement. Angela was really lonely, you know, when Chris was away. Her life and soul of the party, into everything was just a front. She was used to getting her own way."

Time passes as Caroline's life gets back to normal. She is sitting drinking coffee, one morning, thinking how lucky she is. She has got Nick and the girls. She had lost her best friend but, she was gradually joining in with the Mums set. Perhaps Angela had held her back. She didn't have to compare herself, anymore. There was a knock at the door.

"Hello Caroline, may I come in?"

"Yes, James but."

"It's ok. I am not here to take you to bed. I think that you have had enough excitement, recently," James laughed.

"Come in. I'll make another coffee. I've just had one. No more daytime wine for me."

"I have news on our blackmailing. Remember, well how can we forget. Paul was blackmailing us and we didn't think, well at least you didn't, that it was for the money. You told the DCI and, you were right. He wasn't having affairs with any women, we are convinced of that, after interviewing the woman on the estate. He hated women having affairs."

"He was having an affair. He was taking someone else's husband," shouted Caroline, standing up for her friend.

"Yes, he was but, there were no children involved. No children to get hurt. When he was young he was hurt when a family that he had grown fond of was torn apart by the mother having an affair. His own family life wasn't ideal so this was his adopted family. That's strange how we found that out. We got an anonymous call at the station from a woman. It was an untraceable mobile. She said she knew Paul when they were children. We did manage to trace his father. He lives in an old people's home, the other side of the country. He has dementia and didn't remember who Paul was. A shame. The home did tell us that his step mother had died a long time ago. Paul Robertson really didn't have anyone, well, except for Chris, of course. After this, he became a loner. He was determined to stay that way until he met Chris. He had always wondered why he never found women attractive, the way that his work colleagues had. Well, that's the impression we got after talking to old colleagues. We think that he had never had a gay relationship, though. Well, back to the money. He was going to give it to a charity for children from broken homes. We found details of the charities amongst his paperwork. You will never believe this but, the amount that he was going to donate to them is the exact amount that he got from us. The good news is that we will get our money back. We could never work out the significance. He just never got the chance. There is something else."

"Yes, what's that?"

"This is my big confession."

"Go on, I'm intrigued," said Caroline.

"I'm ashamed and its serious. You know that Angela got the rope, that she used, from Nick's garage?"

"Yes, I must admit, I had forgotten that day when she asked for that. Daft of me especially, as the police wanted to know who had access to the garage. I could probably have saved Nick earlier."

"This is the bit that's hard for me to say. Angela and I tried to implicate Nick. We both wanted to blame him for the murder."

"What?"

"Yes, I know. Two people who cared for you were trying to hurt you by taking your husband away. I'm not proud."

"Why."

"Well, I wanted you for myself. That's all. I was trying to get Nick out of the way. Angela, well that's obvious, she was trying to protect herself."

"She was my friend. How come that you two colluded?"

"She met me one day and told me that you would be better off with me and that you wanted to leave Nick."

"She did what?"

"I, obviously, didn't know at the time that she was the murderer, did I? I was stupid. I thought that I wanted you and the girls."

"I can't believe this," Caroline was now sobbing with anger.

"I know that Angela was only trying to protect herself but, I do think that she really did care for you. She did tell me that she was jealous of our affair. I suppose that was because she couldn't attract Paul and had lost Chris, as well."

"Even if I can believe that Angela killed Paul and betrayed me, there is something that I just can't accept. I mean, Paul was going to ruin her life, her brilliant life. I even believe that she never meant to kill him but, and this is the big but, she wouldn't kill Viv. Poor little Viv. She wouldn't hurt a fly. Angela wouldn't do that."

"Angela knew that Viv could also ruin her life. She knew that she was getting close to finding out that Chris was Paul's lover."

"It's ironic, really," said Caroline, hugging her coffee cup.

"What is?"

"Angela was the one who was desperate to find out information on Paul's love life. I'm convinced that Viv would have kept quiet, if she had found out that it was Chris. I don't think that she would upset Angela. She probably would have told Ryan and kept it to themselves. She wouldn't have told Yvonne. No, I'm sure that she thought too much of Angela. She would have been shocked but, kept quiet."

"There is one more thing. You know that I was taken off the case. The boss knew about you and me. You know that. I think that he also knew that I was trying to frame Nick. This is a lot to ask but, if you never mention this to anyone, I get to keep my job. I shouldn't ask this of you but, I think that I will always love you, Caroline, in my own strange way. If you help me you will never have to see me again."

"My family life and new found peace of mind mean so much to me. I may have lost you and my best friend but, yes I will keep your secret. No more excitement for me. My good fortune is that Nick never found out about us. If he did he never said a word."

"Just one more thing, before I go. Just to lighten the mood, if possible."

"Yes, James. What?"

"Well, you know the Chief Inspector always thought that the vicar, that weird helper of his and the pub landlord were acting suspiciously?"

"Yes, they weren't in on the murder, were they?"

"No, nothing like that. The weird bloke and the vicar were making wine and the pub was selling it. Of course, this is illegal but, they were raising money for poor families in the village."

"I knew that they were up to something. I hope you and your boss haven't put them off."

"Oh, there's something else."

"Something else? Don't tell me that Angela has committed more crimes."

"No, this has nothing to do with Angela, Paul, the vicar or illicit alcohol sales. Twenty five years ago there was another murder in Barker's End. We were in our teens and probably didn't take a lot of notice. Too busy doing whatever teenagers were supposed to be doing. Well, I probably remember, you know, wanting to join the police. I vaguely remember that the murder was never solved."

"Yes, you're right. I don't remember it, at all."

"Anyway, the boss, Alan Stock, has solved that one as well."

"Really, how and why?"

"He had to see if there was a connection with that and the murder of Paul Robertson. It could have been a serial killer who only strikes in the village every twenty odd years. Highly unlikely but, a detective can never rule anything out. The boss compared DNA and it turns out that it was her husband all along. He was the only person arrested at the time."

"Have they arrested him now?"

"No, it turns out that he died in Australia, years ago. Of course, no one will ever know his motive."

"Well. What do you know? All of the mysteries solved. I am going back to my quiet life. I am just going to enjoy my family. I do miss Angela, of course. Mysteries, murders and affairs were never really me. Thanks for coming, James, bye."

Caroline was now going to lead the quiet life she was used too.

Angela was watching the small television in her prison cell. News of her crimes was still being mentioned on the local news. It's still about me, she thought. All about me.

THE END

Lightning Source UK Ltd.
Milton Keynes UK
UKHW010630140422
401564UK00001B/133